# EDEN ON EARTH

DHAVAL SONSOIL

ISBN: 978-0-6456762-1-1

# Introduction

*What is life all about? Why are we struggling in this majestic world? What to make of tragedies, difficult situations, circumstances, and setbacks? Why do we see so much hatred, violence, wars, and suffering in this world? Why can't we fix this world for everyone to live in peace and prosperity?*

*Why don't we have what we need? Why do we get attached to everything around us? Why do we hold on to more than what we need? We are supposed to celebrate life every moment, but here we are, struggling to live, and the world is struggling to hold its people together!*

*We are truth seekers. We aim to raise awareness amid chaos and disconnection and nudge the world toward harmony with nature. We write not just for the person who loves literature but for the dispossessed, the lonely, the poor, the rich, the weak, the powerful, and the numb. We are a collaborative team who lives by the motto of "I am because we are."*

*The alter-ego of Dhaval Sonsoil is fictitious and, therefore, a persona that belongs to all of us. We seek to bring readers into a profound, enticing world of fiction that will entertain, inform, and awaken. In doing so, we hope to spark a new interest in spirituality without any self-improvement fluff and an understanding that nature and love are more important than money and power over others. We hope to spark a movement toward genuine wisdom beyond religion and dogma.*

*We have experienced Eden on Earth for the last five and half years and celebrate every day of our life. Every word in Eden on Earth is from beyond us; therefore, our passion lies in bringing this special message, "celebrate life in every moment of life," to our audience and everyone in this wonderful world. We hope every word will touch your heart and transforms you truly to celebrate life.*

# *Table of Contents*

# CHAPTER 1 TRUTH

I always thought enlightenment was no more than a fairy tale. I assumed that to achieve it, one had to grow old in a mountain cave, meditate under a Bodhi tree, or be delirious enough to hear the sound of one hand clapping. Now I have come to realize that it's something much simpler. Enlightenment is just another word for love, true and selfless love that enables people to experience joy in all situations in every moment of their life.

And yet, love has become a dirty word. Many will tell you it's complicated and messy, that it gets sticky, that it distracts you from purity, that it can be done right, and it can be done wrong. Others will tell you that love is a chemical process in the brain and nothing more. And if you search for it any more profound than that, you'll be waiting for a long like a person waiting to hear the sound of a tree falling in a forest that makes no sound.

And, yet, if you ask any two random lovers—I'm talking about the true lovers, not the Hollywood or Bollywood version, but two lovers that eat at each other's snot and scent each other's breath, who want to be in each other's skin, not just be with each other—about enlightenment. They'll tell you they don't care. As far as they're concerned, they've already found the answer, and it's this: all you need is true and selfless love. That kind of love makes lovers feel content to stay with each other in every moment of their life, run through deserts and sail oceans, and climb mountains, because what else is there worth finding? They've experienced what they've been looking for, the joy of living, experiencing the depth of love, the catalyst, the glue that binds all creation from time immemorial, now and forever.

If I sound like a guru, I'm not. I was confused not just by love, but by life itself for most of my life. Sure, I read about enlightenment in books and saw it mentioned in films. Sometimes it was called moksha, illumination, and other times an ecstasy pill. Some others called it living joyfully every day without any worries for tomorrow! But either way, it was always something cryptic, an abstract idea people threw about at meditation retreats, seminars, and in 'spirituality' or 'austerity' or 'postmodern art' workshops, but inevitably made at least one person feel uneasy because big words meant significant opinions.

Would enlightenment mean having an encyclopedia inside your head? Or was it more a case of being able to project the past and the future like a film reel of dinosaurs and nebulas upon the back of one's mind? Or, then again, was it more an aesthetic thing? A glowing halo and a white tunic? Was that all it was? Just an image? A pretense? Or knowing and understanding how to live a joyful life at all times in all circumstances? Is it an idea of something that didn't exist but people clung on to because of sheer fear, fear of being a conscious presence in a universe that is nothing more than a black vacuum of black holes and giant spinning orbs, one of which we found ourselves stuck to, thanks to that miraculous and very convenient force we call gravity?

But I was never interested in what others wanted to tell me about enlightenment. I wanted to see it for myself. You know, I've always only ever wanted the truth. Absolute, not relative truth. Black coffee, no sugar truth, truth beyond illusion. Release from insanity. Release from chaos. Freedom from daily pain, struggles, and disappointments of life—release from greed for power and wealth. Escape from intolerance, violence, and desires of the world.

Did I find it? I'll let you be the judge. Because who am I to tell you what you should think anyway? Who am I to tell you what the meaning and purpose of your life are? Too many people in this world are convinced they have the answers. The world has become too loud, too distorted to hear gentle and absolute truths. I don't think you'll believe what I have to say even if I do tell you. You have to see it for yourself. You have to experience it for yourself! And isn't that the whole idea of the one hand clapping and the tree falling in the forest, making no sound?

The answer is simple. As soon as you try to explain enlightenment or the joyful living in every situation in every moment of life, you have lost it, just like you try to clap with one hand, but you will not make a sound.

All I can tell you is my story.

# CHAPTER 2 CHILDHOOD

I was born on a cool autumn day in Bangalore on November 1st, 1984. And, if the bestowing of a name indicates the desired character, I was named Dhaval Sonsoil. Dhaval means 'pure' in Hindi, so my parents hoped I would grow up complete and virtuous. A cool breeze blew through the city that day, carrying wafts of cumin and fennel. It was a joyous day, and the hospital resounded with people talking, whispering, and singing. Indeed, any stranger who might have encountered this commotion could be forgiven for thinking I was born with a halo around my head. But no, I was born as the son of wealthy, well-known parents. And that last one, the singing part, you don't have to be born a prophet to do that in India. As my Aunt Vidya used to say, "Never trust a god who doesn't dance or sing." And as any Hindu sees god in every sentient being, you might begin to understand how one only gets so far in India with two left feet.

Of course, I don't remember the day I was born because that's impossible, but my parents, grandfather, and aunt have told me enough stories in rich detail, so I feel I can remember them. On the day of my birth, the city was gripped in shock and grief by the massacre that followed the death of Indian Prime Minister Indira Gandhi. But my

Aunt Vidya used to say that there was something magical about that day. On that day, everyone stopped by that room and came in; the midwives, the janitors, and everyone came to see me. It was as if I were something extraordinary.

If I close my eyes, I can imagine the beeping of hospital machines, the flickering lights, and the softness of warm linen wrapped around me. I can imagine my mother holding me in her arms tightly against her chest. Her blurred face is in Tetris shapes of black and white. Her voice was not muted by flesh and water but free to swim in the air all around me, that soft cooing lulling me to return to the womb of sleep—that warmth. I still imagine it like a seed planted in my chest, slowly spreading out like a liquid into my lungs and breath, curling up into the inner delta of my heart. Such is the power of imagination.

What was my first memory?

I spent the first eight years of my life growing up in a large house situated just off a busy road in the upper hills of Bangalore. It was a pretty house in a simple but charming way. It was two-storeyed, double brick, with a white door right in the front, making it quirky for all its symmetry. Strapped around it like twine were numerous vines which in summer would become so luminous that they seemed to glow bright green, and in the breeze, they would shiver like dragon scales. Not the scales of dragons you see in typical fantasy books, but scales of dragons that look more like the serpent dragons in ancient Chinese mythology that have hardly any arms or legs. Dragons seemed to breathe pretty strands of colorful silk instead of fire.

Along the long driveway that led straight to the white front door planted a row of ylang-ylang trees. In the autumn, their petals would shower on the concrete in little white trails that looked like cirrus clouds that had accidentally sprouted from the ground, not knowing they were supposed to be in the sky. When they fell, they would lend such a delicate, sticky, vanilla-like sweetness to the air.

My childhood was much like many young Brahman boys—the richest colors, the familiar scents of lime, cumin, rose, ginger, and turmeric, bursts of laughter, wailing, warm hugs, and spicy curries. Though I was an only child, I was always surrounded by family, my parents, of course, my grandfather, at least in the first five years of my life before he passed away, and my Aunt Vidya, who was a widow as her husband Nikesh had passed away before I was born. My father's family loved me and welcomed my mother wholeheartedly into their culture. They even taught her to dance in Bollywood style. She was pretty good at it too.

If the scent had color, my mother would have appeared surrounded by a cloud of amber, as the sweet smell of maple seemed to be the natural perfume of her skin. Anyone would have seen quite quickly that my mother was a foreigner in those parts. Her name was Bethany, her skin was fair, and she had dark brown hair that glowed copper when caught by the sun. When she was in a good mood, she wore shiny, peach-red lipstick, the kind I imagined a classic actress like Katherine Hepburn would have worn, and she would go to the lounge room and dance, not in any particular style, but her style, the style of 'no one watching.'

The thing I remember most about my mother is her eyes. They were a light turquoise with a deeper lapis lazuli blue at the outer rims, the blue in which Iranian mosque domes are painted to mimic the sky and become doorways to Heaven. It wasn't just something I noticed. Everyone knew it. And no one even had to say about it. You could see people falling into those eyes when they met my mother. When you look into those vivid blue eyes, you feel as though you can see the goldfish swimming in the blue supernova ponds of her mind where only the innermost, sacred secrets of the universe live. It was those deep blue eyes that always seemed to bore down into my soul every time she looked at me, and in those early years, I regret to say there were times when I grew to resent them, for they were the reason I could never tell a single secret to my mother. Any time I caused the slightest bit of mischief, like, when I was caught drawing crayons on the wall or when I walked with muddy feet in the hall, she would shout down the hallway by my full name, "Dhaval Anas Gama Sonsoil, you come here right this minute!"

I would show up sheepishly in the kitchen, the heart of any good home. All my mother had to do was look at me with the mosque-blue eyes, and I would confess every mischief I ever daydreamed of committing as if I were hypnotized.

When I was a good boy, though, she tended to call me Dave, which coincidentally meant 'God' in the Konkani language, my father's native tongue. Father was happy because, as a Hindu, he believed that everyone and everything was God. "Our little Dave, our little God!" he would say. After many years the nickname stuck.

My father was a towering presence. For most young boys, their father will always seem imposing, for we tend to look at our parents as gods, another race of being, when we are young. How can we ever be as big as them, we think? Or indeed, we don't even think about it. My father was a strong man, a big man. At that young age, everything about him seemed significant to me. He had big arms, shoulders, ears, teeth, and wide-set open eyes. Even his voice was big, and I often heard it booming at home even when he wasn't talking to me. It was the kind of voice that penetrated walls. I always imagined that father would have been a terrible spy for that very reason. He was just too big. If he ever had tried to hide behind a wall in James

Bond style in a nuclear testing facility in an attempt to steal nuclear codes, he would have drawn more attention than glowing uranium.

# CHAPTER 3 GENETICS

My mother and father were very different in appearance; I guess that's why I was pretty average in most respects. I was neither big nor small, neither dark-skinned nor fair. I inherited my mother's bright blue eyes but not her white skin. I inherited my father's jet-black hair and tanned skin but not his physical size. Anyone who had seen my mother and father with me would have thought they had kidnapped me because I looked in the exact middle of their appearances and didn't look like either. Because my parents were so different, many people would have questioned how they had ever met. They looked different. They even sounded different. My father was such a big man, and my mother was a petite woman from Florence Beach, California. But such is love.

Mother had first come to India in the 1970s following the wave of interest in India at that time, fuelled mainly by The Beatles tour leading up to the White Album when George Harrison started taking sitar lessons from Ravi Shankar and John Lennon claimed that meditation was so good that he was never touching drugs again. She was interested in the new age spirituality, Krishnamurti and Osho, the idea that every answer to the world's problems could be found if we returned to the ancient teachings in

Mother India. She was part of the San Francisco hippy movement and didn't just talk about putting flowers in her hair; she did it.

It was in Bangalore, backpacking around five years before I was born, that she met my father. They met in the Lalbagh botanical garden in central Bangalore when my mother ultimately became utterly lost trying to find the nearby ashram. Stumbling into my father, she asked for directions to the ashram, which father convinced her was closed because the guru had gone insane, stolen a lot of money, and run off to Switzerland, all of which mother later found out to be only half true. He did steal a lot of money but had run off only as far as his beachside condo in Surat. But it didn't matter. By then, father had already invited her to join him for a cup of tulsi tea.

They hit it off. In my father, my mother saw mandalas and namaste, and my mother's father saw yellow taxis and Coca-Cola. But not only did my mother fall in love with my father, but she also fell in love with India. Our family home was not a typical Indian home, even by high-caste standards. Sometimes mother and father cooked together. Sometimes they sang together. Often, they danced, hands on hips or swaying like happy sea anemones to the rhythms of the sitar and tabla.

It was clear to me that they were very much in love.

My father had grown up in a very conservative high-caste family, but there was something different about him. Undoubtedly, that was why he rebelled against the idea of arranged marriage. He always believed in doing what he wanted to do. He was, as I would understand, quite a ruthless businessman too. His presence made it difficult for anyone not to feel intimidated, and I am sure this helped him build his career, though he had quite the head start.

He inherited much of his wealth from my grandfather, including an estate of agricultural land in Mangalore we affectionately called 'Paradise,' where each year bountiful crops were spurred on by the monsoon rains and the sun. But it wasn't just that. There was something magical about that land, for it was always incredibly fertile. Everything in Paradise grew. Sometimes it felt like you had to look sideways at an orchid, and it would bloom right then and there.

Grandfather inherited all of the estates from his father, and the story goes that he was given the land as a gesture of gratitude for saving a British commander's life after a cobra bit the commander in the early days of British settlement. I'm not sure how accurate the story is. Regardless, to my father's credit, he did not just maintain that initial wealth; he built upon it. This was a time when people desired more healthy and leisurely infrastructure. People were no longer content; they wanted to enjoy themselves better than anyone else. They wanted the best. And my father used his capital wisely, investing in new properties for leisure and health care facilities in Bangalore, and eventually, he was seen in those parts as royalty.

And this allowed my mother to live a life of much freedom, which suited her just fine. She was never one to sit down and be a model housewife, just cooking and cleaning. She always did her own thing, and she was proud of it.

As much as the relatives taught mother much about Indian culture and dancing, mother taught them a thing or two. Some days I would find her in the living room dancing to Otis Redding or Van Morrison. Even if she was aware someone was watching, she danced like they weren't there, as if she were in her bedroom, still sixteen years old, hearing Janis Joplin on her HI-FI for the first time. I have always profoundly admired her. The fact that she didn't care. I remember watching her from behind the lounge room door as she danced to Cat Stevens, thinking how dorky she looked. But deep down, I loved her being so.

# CHAPTER 4 PARADISE

In those first eight years of my life, my parents and I would make the winding journey through the Western Ghats to my father's estate every summer. The house was much like a chateau, and it was a large, white, particularly ornate building with seven bedrooms and a large terrace that looked over the entire land and the two large rivers that cut through it.

The place was Paradise. Okay, Paradise Island, if you want to be formal. But nobody ever actually called it that. It wasn't an island but a two-thousand-acre mosaic of green and yellow paddy fields, each side flanked by two snaking rivers.

I remember that place like it was the back of my soul, and I can still see it with my eyes closed. And I mean the littlest things, the subtlest things most people nowadays never pick up, even in photos. You see, some people hung a painting in their lounge for twenty years, and if you asked them what color the trim of the fishing boat in the photograph is, they'd say, "Fishing boat?"

If Paradise Island was a painting, I saw, felt, and marveled at everything. Everything.

I can tell you everything about that spot as if it's still a painting in my mind. Each year this is how it happened. Rains pelted the land, the rains would cease, and the air would smell of earthy moss. Bacteria would release their gases from the soil and stone, the summer sun would fade for the sowing, and ultimately the time of harvest would mark the end of the rainy season. There was motion everywhere! People walking, people working, people talking, children playing. Cows, buffalos, sheep, and chickens walk out from their shelter for the green pasture and grains, running and dancing in the sunshine, playing in the rain, and in the evening, queuing up to return to their large sheds. In the morning, I saw women carrying water from the river back to their huts. Birds returned to the skies and the trees, the clouds returned to the skies too, and the scents of the flowers and the plants returned to the air, fresh and free from the blanket of the rain. Gently, the wet rural areas dried out, readying barns for the fruit of the earth, and slowly but surely, the workers would return to their hard labor.

I can still see how in the early autumn after the rains had passed, the first rays of the new sun would hit the yellow trumpet trees, their cue to release their warm, sweet scent into the air. And in the bright autumn, thousands of acres of paddy fields would turn a yellow so intense that it seemed to rival the beauty of the sun. Suppose you stopped a moment to listen, perhaps walking by the side of a road early one morning or evening. In that case, you'd hear the rustling through the palm fronds of jungle birds. In the early morning, when the mist still hovered above the jungle tops, or in the late evenings when the sky would turn a peach-melon pink, you'd hear the birds chirping and singing to each other stories their parents once sang to them. If you stopped to look, you'd see butterflies and fruit flies filling the air, dancing electrically. If the morning breeze were cooler, you'd feel it in the veins of your hands. The soil was full of life's energy; diving your hands into it, you'd feel the power coursing through your bones. And perhaps, just perhaps, you would have the epiphany that you were nature.

The most stunning sunrise and sunsets would light the sky pink and tangerine in the early mornings and evenings. The air was humid but crisp. In summer, the scents of mangoes and jackfruit wafted in the air from the adjacent jungle that seemed to glow green in my periphery forever, no matter which direction I looked. It was a scent I could have breathed in for all eternity. It was pretty, indeed, Paradise. In the mornings, rare, exotic jungle birds would fly over our mansion, and I would watch them till I could not see them anymore for accidentally staring too much at the sun, trying to follow their beautiful colors. And sometimes, we would see monkeys in the nearby trees hollering, hooting, and swinging from branch to branch, sometimes eating nuts and fruit, sometimes simply playing. It was a world that just invited you to be part of it. The trees lulled me to sleep each day and woke me up with their rustling in the morning breeze. Each day, from the moment I woke up, I wanted to be outside, connected with the world of nature.

# CHAPTER 5 MAGNETISM

The first thing I did each morning was open all the house windows if they weren't open because Aunt Vidya said that was my job.

"What would happen if we just kept them closed?" I asked her.

She said opening all the windows and doors at the start of each day was necessary. "The spirit of the day is like a stranger each day who knocks at your door," she said. "If you don't open it, it will keep walking past, and then there will be no today, and you'll still be living in yesterday. Who wants to live in yesterday? If the spirit of the day didn't arrive, you'd lose touch with the day after that and the day after, and you'd always be days behind."

In short, it was good to let the day's spirit be because the day's heart, as Aunt Vidya put it, was 'good and divine.'

"What if the spirit of the day is bad?" I asked.

"There is no such thing as a bad day," she replied. "Only bad attitudes!"

Mother used to say that she and Aunt Vidya got along like a house on fire, which confused Aunt Vidya at first because she always thought of the house as a home and a home as an individual. When she let the spirit of the new day in, she was also letting the heart of the house out, and though her clothes shone more brightly than the sun, perhaps that's why it frightened her more than the idea of being on fire. Plus, a saying like that only conjured up images of widows jumping on funeral pyres to follow their husbands into the purity of the flame and, thus, into death. I know Aunt Vidya hadn't done that when her husband Nikesh died. India is a land of many cultures, but widows jumping on funeral pyres wasn't part of hers or mine, and if anyone tried to force Aunt Vidya on a funeral pyre, I think she would have punched them clean out. She was a strong woman; she would have given my father a good run for his money. Still, she got what mother meant.

There was something magnetic about Aunt Vidya. I had already decided that I liked her when I was born. She always wore brightly colored saris, and she was always smiling just as brightly as her clothes. Whenever she got excited about something, whether it was the news of a cousin's marriage or the sight of a rainbow, just like her father, she would clap her hands and look up to the sky as praise for the moment before saying, "Divine! Divine! Oh, it is all so very divine!" And there was a lot you could call divine in those years of my life.

Mother didn't just love Paradise; she adored it. In the vegetable garden in front of the holiday home, she planted all kinds of vegetables: tomatoes, beans, chili, potatoes, countless herbs of all varieties, and in the borders around this vegetable garden, she planted neat little lines of pansies, daisies, and peonies. All those plants took care of themselves. Usually, there was no need to water them, and the sun continued to shower them with warmth and light. There was something so magical about that entire process, how the little saplings, so weak and flimsy at first, would mature into tall, spindly stems, and from those stems, leaves would appear, and from the tops of the branches, a bulb and from the bulbs, flowers or fruit. All the plants sparkled in the sunlight after each summer downpour. When tomatoes, beans, and potatoes were all ripe, we would pick and pluck them and cook them into curries to celebrate the summer, but more than that, to celebrate life. Each curry symbolized something beautiful, the end of summer and the start of another journey to the next rainy season (monsoon).

# CHAPTER 6 MEMORIES

Do you know what they say about memories being fake? Our memories are always memories of memories. That wasn't the case with my childhood because I always had photos to document. My mother wasn't necessarily a photography buff, but she had an old Olympus camera with which she would happily roam the garden. Sometimes she'd take photos of family events. You know, the usual stuff. Photos of birthdays, me blowing out the candles on a cake, Aunt Vidya cooking in the kitchen, father in his suit and tie, and carrying his suitcase walking through the door after work. But sometimes, mother would go missing for an hour or two. She'd roam around in the countryside and on long walks through the forest. Often I'd go with her. We never told anyone where we were going or when we'd be back. We'd just go. And mother would always have that camera around her neck. To her, photography was a kind of poetry, and poetry was a kind of photography. Both were the pursuit of capturing moments.

I remember one day, I saw mother walk outside the garden and follow the little stone path that snaked down into the jungle, and I called out to her, "Don't forget me!"

She didn't hear me until I ran after her, and the sound of my heavy feet made her turn around. "Dhaval?" she said.

I followed my mother through the trees I imagined were gnarled, crooked, bark people reaching their hands out to the sky. I dawdled behind, and after being distracted by watching squirrels scurrying up a tree, I looked around. I couldn't see my mother or hear her. Did she have the magical power to turn invisible, like Mr. India? I wondered. Everything glowed a bright luminescent green. I ran through the trees, and the leaves fell and swirled around in circles. Where was I? I didn't know. The leaves seemed made of silk, the wind of satin. And for a moment, I was lost in it all, and I couldn't differentiate the dream from reality before the birds in a nearby tree suddenly took to the air and started singing as a harsh breeze swiftly blew through. But nothing more.

I stood upon a little patch of dirt overlooking the estate on the highest area of it, where we could see the little creek in the distance and the evening sun mirroring from the glazed buildings of the city in the far distance.

The next moment I saw a bright blue bird gliding across, high in the sky. I traced it fly from the far-off field to the right of our property, disappearing behind the clouds. The bird continued through the sky as if drunk, in fits and wobbles; it seemed an epic struggle to keep itself aloft, sometimes more falling than flying, then hoisting itself back into the sky in perpetual loops.

I took off following the bird, running as fast as my legs could, but I wasn't used to running and was not used to extreme physical activity. However, I came across a peacock I had seen eating a fine apple. The peacock ran straight into the jungle, and without thinking, I ran straight into it, colliding with trees and leaves and smashing my way through the forest growth like a drunken rhinoceros.

I stopped, momentarily dazed from smacking headfirst into a tree. I shook myself off and took note of my surroundings. At that moment, I spotted something above me. Again, the bird! An Indian roller, its blue feathers gleaming in the sunlight. It circled me a little further up the path briefly before the bird fell from the sky as if hit by an invisible bullet and, in a flutter of feathers, fell in a straight line to the ground directly in front of me. Overcoming my shock, I did not hesitate to run to it. Finding it based on its back against the dirt, I saw it was still alive. It appeared motionless except for its wide-awake eye, blinking, looking directly at me. At that moment, I stared into that eye and had the strangest sensation: I am you, and you are me. I felt I could feel everything the bird was feeling, and at that moment, I knew the bird could feel everything I was feeling too. I knelt beside it; put my hand on its chest.

I felt drowned in the bird's eyes. It was as if I were staring at myself. I took in every detail of the bird, the beautiful blue feathers, bright turquoise and ultramarine blue. I could see the bird had a broken wing.

I put my hand on its body and felt its tiny heart beating, and I felt that warmth I had felt as an infant. I could not wholly remember it; only the feeling lingered with me. It was only ever feelings. Suddenly the bird, as if escaping from a daze, flapped its wings and got up to its feet as I retreated my hand. It stared at me again for a moment, its cold, black, beady eye drinking into my appearance before it took off again into the sky.

Looking into the bird's eye, suddenly, there was stillness. For that moment, standing there in silence, the colors seemed to become endlessly more profound. Then, far in the distance, I thought I heard voices. A faint lulling song came rustling up the trees, and the dirt, on the wind. The leaves seemed to move slower all of a sudden as if some grand secret of the universe was exposing itself for a moment within the movement of the leaves. Deep, purple shadows filled the gorge, creating mottled shadows that seemed to swirl in the shapes of birds swarming. A blizzard of leaves fluttered around me.

"Dhaval!" called a voice from afar.

# CHAPTER 7 REVOLUTION

Digging my hands into the soil, I watched spiders, ants, centipedes, and everything else crawling over the earth, going about their own lives in their forests of daisies and grass. Like most young kids, I had a billion questions about the world. I looked to see my mother digging with a small shovel in the garden near me.

"Mother, why do birds sing?"

"They sing for the same reason we do," my mother replied. "Because if we didn't sing, we would not live."

"But how do they know their songs?"

"They teach themselves."

"Mother, why do things die?"

"You must be the master of your fate. Look here," she then said. "See this flower? It's a dandelion, yes?"

"Yes," I replied.

"And a dandelion is a flower?"

"Yes," I replied.

"And it is beautiful. You and I both know that well, and everyone thinks they know that well. People write songs about this flower, Dhaval. Songs and poems and people will paint pictures of it and do all kinds of celebration about it. And yet, when they walk through the park, the same people will walk on top of it. They'll walk on top of the thing they love more than anything else. Now, Dhaval, look at the sky."

Mother grabbed my head gently in her hands and redirected my face to the clouds.

"It's beautiful, isn't it?"

"Yes."

"You see, Dhaval, the sky is the most beautiful thing in the world we are ever likely to see. It's so beautiful, but we forget about it. It's so big and ominous, but we forget it's there. The sky is never the same; think of all the eons that have passed, warriors and chariots and pyramids and kingdoms that have risen and fallen. They all did so under this masterpiece. They saw it also—the sky. The same sky, more or less, that we see. And isn't that beautiful? That we could all live under the same sky. Oh, yes. Yes, it is, Dhaval. It is the most beautiful. And yet we don't think of polluting it. The sun rises and lowers in the sky, lighting the entire creation day in and day out from time immemorial, without which no life can sustain on the Earth. And people now will tell you that the sky is different. But the sky is not different, Dhaval. It never was, and it never will be. The sky is everything. It is the void. It is all things into infinity and all things into negative infinity. That is the spirit. Understand?"

"No."

My mother picked the dandelion from the garden, and her golden necklace caught the sun. I had only seen that locket opened twice, and even then, only from afar. I knew what was inside it from peeking into it once when it was left on the foyer counter. It was a small photo of my mother wearing a yellow chrysanthemum dress. She looked as gorgeous today as she was in that photo as she held the dandelion in front of her and then blew away the seeds to watch them float into the sky.

"People often kill the thing they love."

Mother removed her gloves, wiped her brow, took a long breath, and looked over the landscape, a streak of dirt brandishing her forehead. It was as if she felt more at rest, more sitting in the joy of her soul, and each time she would say the same thing, "Isn't this Heaven, Dave?"

She always said heaven was right there amongst that plot of land. It was there in the river, in the trees, in the wind, in the neighborhood; all we had to do was realize it, open our eyes and see it, open our ears and hear it and live our lives loving, caring, and sharing to the fullest to experience it. And take that love to the people around us to live in communion and experience heaven.

"This is it, Dave," she would say, with a shovel in her hands and gardening gloves covered in dirt. "This is EDEN." And I would dig my hands back into the rich soil in some newly turned section of the vegetable patch, and in the moments when everything was quiet enough, I would imagine I was feeling the warmth of Earth's heart.

# CHAPTER 8 THE VOID

I grew up before the advent of screens and social media. My charger was the sun, my entertainment was nature, my social media was the birds and the centipedes and the moths and the monkeys and everything in between, a world of winged and furred beasts fluttering or howling or gliding through my days and nights in the jungles, cicadas humming and kestrels tapping at my window. There was no need to like something because it would have been absurd to say you didn't like something. And my screen? My screen was the sky. In the day, it screened daylight blue; at night, it played the stars.

After each summer trip to Paradise, my mother, father, and I would pack our things each time; I would complain that I never wanted to leave. Still, I would inevitably bid goodbye to Aunt Vidya and the vegetable garden, the centipedes and the ants, and we would start our long trip back to Bangalore. Each year it was the same routine. Father would get in a huff and puff about being late for our return to Bangalore and some business detail, and mother would always forget something. Always. The last summer, we were all in Paradise; I remember she forgot her purse and had to run inside to get it.

I remember that day; the sunlight streamed through the car windows like thin golden ribbons through the trees' thick, yellow, brown, orange, and green foliage. We went through the Western Ghats, among the planet's wealthiest rainforests. It's a massive amount of land stretching 1,600km along India's West Coast, from Gujarat to the southern tip of Kerala. I was often told that countless animals lived in those rainforests; tigers, leopards, the enigmatic black panther, and wild Asian elephants, but I only ever saw the elephants. As we drove on, sometimes we would see the elephants through the trees; other times, we passed some laborers working along the roadside, and I remember seeing their chiseled faces and bare chests and thinking they looked exhausted. I snapped out of my revelry for just a moment.

"Mother, why does the Earth spin?"

Mother turned around from the passenger seat to look at me and smile. I remember that beautiful Heaven-blue of her eyes as she turned around to speak to me, "Did I ever tell you, Dave, about the glowing forest?"

"Please tell me," I replied.

I saw for a moment a glimmer in her eyes I knew too well, for it was the same spark in her eye that preceded the story's start. "During monsoon season, the rain-drenched jungles of the Western Ghats can give off an eerie glow, allowing a rare glimpse into one of nature's spectacular eccentricities. And do you know why it glows? Because of a fungus! Imagine, the first man who went underwater in a submarine tried to use the wood—"

The glass exploded like powdered snow. At that moment, there was a great howling of metal, the world flipped upside down, and I saw the front of the truck for a brief moment as it swallowed the side of the car. What followed was nothingness. And I mean void, like the nothingness I imagine most coma patients experience—sheer nothing.

Then a speck of light. An ember is floating through a vast vacuum of space against a backdrop of nothingness. It was so faint at first, so fast, it seemed to disappear as soon as it had appeared. The void, in the form of that mysterious sensation that can only be felt, washed over me like an ocean over a grain of sand. And then! Again! That glimmer! A single speck, a single dot, a pixel of light, blinking so faint, I thought it must be a universe away, a single ember still drifting from a long-forgotten fire of a universe that had long ago met its end, floating like the first atom of all creation. I focused on it; I willed sensation upon it, thought upon it, and breathed on it as if breathing on fire. I watched it swell like charcoal, turning a hot blue in a breeze. As I watched it float, I felt myself floating with it, less spinning now, more drifting, as if we were quantum particles, that this mysterious pixel and I were twins, entangled, dancing together, knowing the steps as if we had done this dance before. As we drifted, I saw this ember start to trace a blue line behind it as if its light never faded, and I saw this line of light swell as if it were an ember caught by a camera on prolonged exposure. A string! The string continued to wobble and drift, and I saw it swell as if it were flowing from a paintbrush stirred through the water. The paint rushed till it was wide and flat, and I could see it was now shining faintly as if it were an elaborate silk ribbon flowing behind the hand of some Olympian acrobat running through space, forever dancing.

# CHAPTER 9 LOVE

Love!

We've all heard the word repeatedly in everyday life, in movies, music, and television, so often that we convince ourselves we know what it means. Every guru and self-help coach loves to spout it. They'll talk to you about self-love, divine, platonic, spiritual, charitable, and romance. It makes you feel uncomfortable. Because eventually, you become numb to it. It's like saying a random word over and over again. At some point, it loses all meaning. It becomes cliche.

You start thinking roses and chocolates are love. You start thinking Valentine's Day is love. You start believing love is a thing that can be touched, defined, and quantified. But those things are just symbols we've been told to ingest. And the word love, too, is no different. Every word is nothing more than a symbol. A grasping at essence. A sound of a written form. That's all.

The truth is love takes multiple forms. What is the love of family compared to the love of friends compared to the cultivated love of oneself? Love is all these things and, at the same time, nothing. It is intangible and yet tangible.

But love is not its word. Love is not its label. If you have to explain love, you don't understand it. Epic poets try, but even that act of poetry or song is still grasping. And that's what makes it beautiful.

Love is something you feel, but somewhere along the line, our first forgetting was this idea that the bird existed before we called it a bird, that the flower existed before we called it a flower, that the universe existed before we called it the universe. There is no such thing as a bird or a flower in the universe. To the universe, there is no such thing as love. There is only one thing that exists beyond the word. An essence. An ethereal something.

Through the years of our lives, we try desperately to understand it, let it go, catch it, and hold it. We devote our entire lives to the challenge. And then one day, all this great big thing that changes our lives forever with the weight of the world comes down to one last moment of sight where you come face to face with the thing that you feel, the thing beyond words, the thing that always was and always will be, the item you knew was there, but you didn't want to look at it.

The void.

And in that moment of what I looked back on as my death, it was not emptiness, for emptiness is a thing, and I can only call it the void. It was seeing into the infinite of the infinite. I could never explain it in terms of sight, sound, or other stimuli, for there were no such things. It was something I could only feel. I was suspended, forever turning as if still in that car sent flipping by that rogue truck, set to spin like mother said all things spin, eternally, to the ends of the universe.

There are no words to describe the heart-swelling love of a friend or a family member. But there are also no words to describe moments, for some moments in life can't be explained. Aren't they moments of enlightenment?

I saw that last vision of my mother before the accident; I remember it so clearly because it has existed from that moment till now. She exists. Because everything exists. And I know that. But right there and then, I didn't know. All was eternal, all was pain, all was sorrow, and all was despair. And I was alone, faced with the ultimate, beyond words.

# CHAPTER 10 SORROW

The funeral occurred in an old, stone Christian church in Mangalore. I remember walking down the graveyard through the headstones that stood erect and proud, past others covered in damp and speckled lichen and slumping into the grass as if ready to join their owners in the soil. Inside the building, motley light shone through large, stained glass windows. All the sights were terrifying, the image of Christ on the cross, and paintings of blood and flesh of Christ, that seemed to me belonged in some horror film. Before that, I had only seen images of gods as elephants and goddesses with multiple arms. Again, Aunt Vidya's words returned to me, "Don't trust any god that doesn't dance." And I remember looking at that image of Jesus on the cross, thinking what he would think of, that the idea the church chose was the most important thing to remind people of.

But had Jesus danced? Did he, too, I wondered, see what my mother had once seen; that the Earth spins because if it didn't, it wouldn't know what to do with itself, that the bird sings because if it didn't, it wouldn't know what to do with itself? Perhaps Jesus danced, I thought to myself. Perhaps he sang. Perhaps he spun. Maybe that's why he seemed to make a lot of people angry. But I was young. Thus was the simplicity of my ideas.

My father remained stone-faced throughout the funeral, resolute and numb as if making an impression of the sad, naked man on the cross. The whole time he clutched a gold locket around his neck. He was worried he might never be able to picture her face again. No memory could ever recreate her. Forever she was gone. Aunt Vidya wept, embraced my father and me, and the three of us held each other in that final moment.

Until that day, my father, stern as he was, had always been the man you could depend on to fill a room with the sound of relentless observations, anecdotes, and humor. He was the kind of man who kept you intrigued and made you wonder what shade his eyes turned when he was alone in a quiet space in his thoughts. But now his eyes were as cold and grey as we gathered around the grave to watch the coffin lower; the wet wind blew his hair in ironically dramatic tussles. Even when the final song of the service played, my father's eyes remained glassy and cold. He refused to cry. Even as the amplifiers played out,

"When life has ended and my time has run out

My friends and my loved ones, I'll leave. There's no doubt

But there's one thing for sure when it comes my time

I'll go this old world with a satisfied mind."

Now for the first time in my life, I was confronted with the knowledge that my mother, the person I had turned to for all my learning in life, had disappeared. I struggled to make sense of what death even was. Wasn't there something, an antidote, some miraculous machine that could save her? If she disappeared, wouldn't she reappear behind her hands in a matter of moments, saying "peek-a-boo"? I didn't want to believe in death. I didn't know how to deal with it. It was too heavy, too abstract, too unknown. There was no cure, remedy, or new Paradise to run to.

"Ashes to ashes, dust to dust," the priest said as the final layers of dirt were thrown upon my mother's grave.

And that was it. She was finally at rest in the Indian soil she had so loved.

My father thanked the funeral-goers as they left the service. They all said the same things, like "Lovely service" or "She is in a better place," but it was clear words could only do so much. All the while, I never saw father shed a single tear. He bottled up the sadness deep inside the seed of his soul, and I knew that even then.

People often talk about love at first sight. You don't often hear about love at the fifteenth sight, or the twenty-sixth sight, or the five-thousand-and-eighty-fifth sight. Rarely do you hear people talk about love at last sight. Because who can? Once you're gone, you're gone. Sometimes I wondered what my last word to my mother was, the last sight. I remembered it all. That look in her eyes just before the truck hit the car.

That last vision of my mother will forever stick in my mind. Those colors will never fade, for that polaroid is laminated. And that image was an image of freedom. She was free at that moment. The wind was blowing through the open car window, she was smiling, the sun was lighting her cheek, and her hair was dancing in the wind. That was the last moment she was still conscious, still here on planet Earth, still thinking, feeling. And I witnessed at that moment something in her eye, some color change in her iris that told me she had seen what I had seen without seeing it; in a split moment before her death, she knew it. That was the awakening. That was when I saw it. Enlightenment happens to everyone. It's just that for most people, it happens at that last moment just before you die.

You laugh because there's nothing else to do. After all, you realize that you were dreaming and awake all at once, and why shouldn't life and death be anything else but the same?

Now my father was alone in the world. I knew it. He knew it. And he looked sad, his eyes grey, his head hanging in perpetual despair. I couldn't bear to see him like that. I wanted to see my parents again. I wanted to see them together. It didn't make sense to see only father now in such a state. My parents had only ever made sense together.

The last time I had seen them both together before we got in that car was when they were both fast asleep in the living room in Mangalore in their armchairs, with the grandfather clock still ticking that had lulled them to sleep, and with their fingers still lightly clinging together to form an 'M.' I had stood there for a good few minutes just taking in sight and knowing that any moment that the last finger would lose touch, making their arms hit the ground, and they would both wake up from their dual sleep.

I thought, in some ways, that's what love was – a brief occasion in the universe of two beings gracing fingers through the blank, eternally expanding nothingness of space before returning to that nothingness again.

# CHAPTER 11 DEATH

When I'm frank about it, I think up until my mother's funeral, I had only understood death as an abstract concept. I had seen in Paradise some of the big juicy tomatoes would not be picked in time before the birds pecked holes in them or they dropped to the ground and wilted, but I never lamented it for each year more tomatoes would grow. But unlike tomatoes, I would never have another mother. Now there would be no more fruit garden, no more dancing; my life would be no longer poetry.

Each week, empty bottles of whiskey, rum, and vodka piled up by the back door before Aunt Vidya would dump them into the garbage. In the evening, I heard father play mother's old records, and I would fall asleep to their sound, imagining mother was still alive, still laughing as she spun like a whirling dervish in the lounge room, still dancing like no one was watching to Van Morrison and Otis Redding.

Meanwhile, I couldn't sleep. Sometimes I wanted to throw up. Otherwise, I wanted to do nothing, even though I wasn't so sure about it. I wanted not to exist, but I also dreaded the thought of non-existence. I felt tired even after sleeping. I felt cold even in the sun. I found myself lying on the floor of my bedroom for long periods, staring at my ceiling. All I could see was my mother. Even staring at the blank walls, I could still see her face. That blue. Those heavenly, blue eyes. All the memories of her flooded back through my heart, in and out again, like an eternal pumping storm. All I could think about was my hands in that rich soil, the caterpillars, ants, and spiders crawling over my skin. But the blissful ignorance of my childhood was gone. Now, sinking my hands into the soil in the front garden, I felt no longer the pulsing heartbeat of the Earth, only dirt.

"Dhaval is sick," Aunt Vidya told my father. "He is upset. He speaks to no one. He stays in his room."

I considered myself dead and a ghost in a world of spirits, a world of limbo forever broken and devoid of meaning.

Because when mother died, everything died. When I looked over the balcony of the house, I saw the plants I once tended to, now limp or dried by the sun, or not there at all, or strangled by the wild mint, which was still in the process of forming an empire over a clutter of boundary rocks.

From that balcony, though, I could see all of Paradise. The sun, the tangerine clouds, the rain. For many days I sat there to look over Paradise. I sat there each day to watch the sunset each night, painting the bright sky purple, orange, and blue.

Looking into the distance, I marveled at the jigsaw puzzle fields and a few random birds flying over a scattering of clouds. I was stunned for a moment by the beauty of the sweeping countryside. The horizon, like a fine thread, now beige white, hovered over the fields before me, over a small beaten track that ran towards the river below. In the distance, the sun painted the sky white and purple. The fields seemed to be brushed back and forth like velvet by some invisible wind.

The sun was burning hot, but there was a cool breeze. On that terrace, I watched nature in the form of trees, that magnificent wind, the tangerine sunsets, and the bees swarming around me. I slowly felt myself synchronizing with the rhythm of nature. I felt the world slowing down and speeding up simultaneously as if my entire world was a time-lapse. The agricultural land turned yellow to amber, amber to ochre, and ochre to green, and flowers bloomed from buds and wilted to do it all again. Frogs croaked here and there; birds shuffled in their canopies.

How happy and oblivious the outside laborers all seemed to me then! The tractors in the distance moved beyond the yellow paddy fields to the edge of the distant river. It seemed it was getting too dark for the laborers to see, and they had now hauled in their plows. Then the noise of the low-caste little children came to be in bits and fits as sound does over distance. I heard them laughing, jumping, and clapping their hands as their parents near the end of the working day. I watched these children playing cricket or tag, reveling in a wealth I could not have: nature, freedom, spontaneity, and fun. Those kids seemed to belong to a completely different world in which they had no reason to care about the mud and the dirt on their clothes. Meanwhile, my world was of status, silk, sequins, and mirrors.

They lived a different life from mine, the men with bare chests glistening in the sun, the women in long shawls. The kids had dirt in their hair, soil, and grit in their hands. In the morning, the women washed clothes in the river, cooked their food in pots in the open air, and shared everything amongst the groups in the huts. When they weren't working, the men thatched the roofs when they needed repair or slept under trees. There was something I envied about low-caste children's world: their sense of connection to the land. I watched them playing with each other happily, though I could barely hear them. I watched the ball thrown back and forth and listened to their laughter. All the time, I wondered what it would be like to be out there, playing with those children of that lower caste. Despite all my family's riches, I was a prisoner in my own home, a home I had once thought housed love but now only seemed to accommodate memories of what had been and what could have been.

No matter how often I told myself she was gone, some part of my mother remained. I didn't believe it. I didn't think she could be gone. Wasn't she there with me just days ago? Wasn't she real in front of me? Couldn't I hear her voice? Couldn't I feel her presence? Sometimes, sad, I would walk through the garden. I would sit at the hill's edge near the house as though waiting for her. I thought maybe, like the tomatoes the birds plucked, a seed of her, an essence of her, would return, plant itself in the soil of life again, and appear before me just like she ever was. And I would ask her questions, and she would tell me of the world, and recite poetry, and dance so unashamedly in the lounge room again, and we would take photos, and she would teach me everything I needed to know about the world that no one else seemed to want to teach me. Or maybe they just couldn't.

# CHAPTER 12 FEAR

I was startled by the sound of smashing glass. As I put my ear to the doorframe, I heard my father shouting at some employees. It was becoming more common for him to get so angry that he would smash things in the house. He always seemed angry with the workers. Rumour started spreading that he was not treating his workers well and that they were due payment. It frightened me.

I was hiding behind the door when I accidentally dropped a glass bottle, and it smashed to the ground, father heard it, and I saw that he had heard it, for he came to me instantly.

"Dhaval?" he said. "Dhaval! You bastard!"

Aunt Vidya got in front of him, "Mister, please! Go easy on the boy!"

I ran outside as fast as my legs could take me. Further and further, I ran into the forest until I was sure I was lost.

I slowed down to walk to catch my bearings. The sun lit the leaves of the trees in a silvery sheen. Everything looked slightly fluorescent. I saw tiny pinpricks of light flashing in the air all around me. I thought it was fireflies, and they were little comets flying overhead, shooting streams of light.

It started to rain. I dashed to a nearby tree and stood under it for a while, watching the rain fall in puddles and muddy the ground. I remember being entranced for a moment by the sound of it, wondering how I would get home before I got drenched. The next thing I remember is seeing what I can only describe as a mirage of a young girl, somewhat my age, as she appeared almost as if out of the sheer darkness of the jungle.

For so long, I had considered myself a ghost, and the world was devoid of magic, but now I was starting to see the magic of reality and life again. And it was nature, and nature was the answer.

Then again! A glimpse of red. A break in the strobing of the light through the trees. I ran through the drizzling rain, keeping the movement of the strobing light just in sight. The water slid against my skin and through my hair, caressing my cheeks like invisible, cold, delicate hands. My feet plodded melodically amid the silence across the wet ground, sending thin, whip-like lashes of water up the backs of my calves as I ran. When I was sure my lungs would burst like Hindenburg into flames, the swaying leaves danced in the cool evening breeze as if electrified, and I saw her again through that curtain. She was moderately tall with dark brown hair cascaded to her waist in beautiful curls, dark, honey-brown, almond eyes, dressed in a half sari and ankle bracelets.

It was as if cupid had shot his arrows straight into the centers of my eyes to blind me with new sight as if Thor had thrown a lightning bolt through the crown of my head to melt me forever to that spot in space and time as if Shakti and Shiva were already dancing up and down my spine. Even at that age, how could I have known what love was? What it meant to be intimate with a woman! What it meant to dance upon the skin of another as if their skin too was silk. I had no idea. All I knew was that something deep in the bottom of my soul fluttered as if nothing had ever beaten me before. In her eyes, I saw the marvels of the universe, I saw the explosions of supernovas, I saw empires built and turn to dust, I saw the blossoming of all life, flowers in perpetual bloom, and the waves of oceans rolling over each other as if the two were cosmic lovers.

I followed the girl, convinced that I must speak to her. I followed the glimpse of her dress through the leaves, following the sound of her steps and movement, but I sensed she was trying to get away from me. I sped up my walking just as I heard her doing the same.

Suddenly there it was again, the bird! All around me, the leaves broke free from their branches and fluttered like scraps of cellophane in a sudden, cosmic wind. I felt incredible warmth envelop me as if the trees and the forest were wrapping me up with their arms around me, like a babe. In the form of one giant spirit of Mother Nature, she hums her ancient lullaby of the melodies she has long sung to the birds, the sun, and the rain.

It's difficult to explain exactly what went through my mind at that moment. A mixture of awe and fear and even bliss? It would be an understatement. It was so exact that it could not wholly be put into words – a feeling, not of loss, regret, or something missing, but something inextricably and miraculously gained. In the core of my entire being, I felt build in my stomach and surge through every pore and every bone of my whole body like electric soul-fire, a sense of profound universal energy that can usually only be found in the plasma of stars.

Suddenly the blue sky, like watercolor, seemed to drip away from itself as if being washed, and the color became fainter till the backdrop of the sky was almost as white as the clouds. Everything else around me, the trees and the house dripped away too and faded into a blank canvas until nothing was white.

I felt myself fall into the ground as if I were a cloud. I felt how the clouds fell on the ground, how the dragon scales looked like dragons. Then I thought about it before I saw it. The glowing orb of light, like an atomic bomb growing and expanding, like an explosion in slow motion. A bubble of light is growing. Brighter. Brighter.Brighter.

# CHAPTER 13 PURITY

Everything around me glowed nuclear white. I felt like I had woken up in the middle of an atomic bomb explosion. I refocused to find that I was now stretched out on a bed in a local hospital. A doctor's face appeared, a floating head in a universe of white. In my ears, I could hear a dull buzz as if they were filled with cotton wool, and on the other side of that cotton wool, someone was scratching steel wool together in an awful attempt to make music. I could see the doctor talking to my father, and though I could make out very little information, I heard the words 'head trauma'. Then, I saw father speaking to me before my brain caught up with the terms, his face crumpled like paper-mâché, as I felt that warmth in the teardrop of my heart grow cool as if the delta of my soul had suddenly dried.

There was the cold and a light pattering of rain.

Aunt Vidya asked me if I remembered how I got there. I said I didn't. I didn't remember any of it. All I remembered was a series of strange dreams. If I wasn't falling, I was levitating. But all the while, I felt that constant sensation in every dream. Of movement. Of spinning. As if I were still in that split second where the car reached the peak of its trajectory in mid-air, being flipped upside down. But how could I explain that? Words would not suffice. These were merely sensations, rarely visuals.

"He was sleepwalking," my father insisted. "That's all."

The doctors gave me medicine; the priests gave me flower garlands. I popped all kinds of pills and Ayurveda remedies, but nothing worked. I still just wanted to throw up. I had vertigo. My vision was blurry. Sometimes I fell asleep, and sometimes I was sure I fell awake. After a while, I couldn't keep track of it. I wouldn't eat anything or drink that day; my skin was itchy. I couldn't sit still. I couldn't sleep for three days in a row.

I kept making up questions all the time I spent in the hospital, in and out of sleep. Sometimes in my delirium, my mind went wild with questions I would never again be able to ask my mother, "Why does the sea look so blue?" And they kept rising. Now my mother was gone, and I felt none of my questions would be answered. I thought in delirium that I would forever walk the world, no longer being able to hold onto a single slither of meaning, like my mind had a gaping hole in it and everything I ever thought I knew had already leaked out. After about nine days, I woke up one morning and again started vomiting.

The next thing I knew, I was lying on a gurney, hooked up to the giant EEG machine's multiple leads, cords, and attachments at a specialist Bangalore hospital. It appeared to be a monstrous machine, a mutant, robotic octopus with limbs and suckers tracing the surfaces everywhere. The doctors ran multiple experiments and filled my brain with liquids they told me glowed on their computer screens and made me think of the glowing wood of the Western Ghats, but though they inspired some ideas in my head, they wouldn't let me see their screens.

They were talking, and I was asking questions and telling them what I knew about my symptoms, but my mind was trying to take me back to my last moments. It was as if I was lying in a cage in a dark room, and a nurse came in and told me to close my eyes, and I did, and I couldn't hear or see anything.

Either I was in the process of waking up or falling asleep. Slowly, like a clockwork toy being serviced, I returned to consciousness again and again, and each time the shock of being in a white hospital room would slowly fade till the white walls were no different from the white walls of my mind. I was numb.

Next, the psychiatrist came. He was a short, stumpy-looking man with spectacles that seemed too small for his head. He had me look at Rorschach's paper, and he told me that I had a personality disorder, and I asked him if I was insane, and he said I wasn't, there was something strange now about my brain, but the depression and stress weren't helping. I don't remember it all, but I know that it was a long process of electroshock, sleeping pills, and medications that made me see Persian rug designs whenever I closed my eyes.

But it seemed there was no cure for the condition.

"We will take him to another specialist," my father said.

"Your son will be mentally handicapped," the specialist replied. "Chances are he won't even be able to walk."

But father insisted they try the most experimental programs, which they keep locked away in a dark filing cabinet at the back of the hospital. The specialists only echoed the same refrain, "There is nothing we can do."

"Don't you know who I am?" roared my father.

"Mr. Sonsoil, I can do nothing for your son."

# CHAPTER 14 HEALING

Aunt Vidya told me the oils would make me feel better. She told me her mother used to do it for her every day, massaging her scalp, and it was an old Ayurveda tradition, she insisted. But the smells of the herbs filled the air around me in wafts and made me a little giddy.

Aunt Vidya was very much into traditional recipes, whereas my father said they were all nonsense. She went to great lengths to force-feed me awful-tasting herbal cures from the tribals in the village. Sometimes, she would bring vials of strange things but never let my father see them. She knew he would get furious if he caught her giving me any of these traditional recipes. She would find times to get me on my own, and she put the situation on me that if I did tell father, there would probably be an almighty fight. So, I knew I had to take these awful "potions," yet I couldn't even make a noise when I did.

I remember one time I was told to take one of these potions. It looked like an orange and had a sort of glittery substance. Aunt Vidya told me I was supposed to drink it on an empty stomach. It tasted like rotting fruit rinds, but Aunt Vidya wouldn't tell me what it was. The night I drank it, I was convinced it was poison, and I gagged. I lay in bed in the dark, shaking with tears, unable to move or speak, unsure if I was going to vomit. I remember hearing the clock ticking in the living room, and I knew it was about five in the morning when my father would get up. I sat up, I opened my mouth, but I could not move. I just lay in the dark, horrified, hoping it would stop soon.

I was not allowed to take even a bath for fear I might drown. And I guess, looking back on it, they were right. It's possible to drown in a puddle if one is talented enough. Talented at death, that is. Indeed, some people are better at dying than others. Some, like the Samurai, were particularly advanced at it, while others were shockingly awful. But some people were just accident prone, my Aunt Vidya said. She admitted that she didn't know yet just how accident-prone I was, for I was not clumsy, I was nonetheless a curious boy, but she saw it in me from a young age. She saw me staring out windows and locked in my daydreaming, playing with insects and bugs outside. She saw it probably better than anyone.

But after all this kind of talk, though I loved my Aunt Vidya very much, I was convinced she was hellbent on killing me, not curing me. Every Ayurveda cure tasted awful, made me feel sick, or both. And I didn't understand that. I wished they would leave me alone. The waking dreams were challenging enough.

Every few days, Aunt Vidya would massage my head with these special oils, and I would tilt my head back in the cane chair on the terrace, staring at the roof of the sky, and she would talk about all kinds of things about her life. Sometimes I think she was taking the opportunity to speak to someone who would listen and didn't know better than to listen. But I would hear. And I cared. Because I always felt that Aunt Vidya cared. And the scalp massage made my brain feel good. It made me calm, and for a bit of a while during those times, smelling the scent of the oils in the hair lotion, I would drift into a dream but for once not feel ashamed for it, or at least not worried that in that space I would see again the nightmare I had seen so many times over and over: the vision of my mother's face, that last look in her eyes before the car flipped.

"You spend a lot of time in the study, reading, yes?" said Aunt Vidya, striking up a conversation as she massaged my head. "You're just like your mother. I understand it."

She took a moment to massage my scalp a little more before rinsing my head with the bit of water she always had.

"Aunt Vidya, do you think mother lives on? I mean, after death?" I asked.

Aunt Vidya chuckled before turning again more severe. "Of course I do, Dhaval. Remember, I believe everything returns to life in some form."

"But," I started. "Mother was a Christian. If she is in Christian Heaven, I would want to be in Christian Heaven, to see her, I mean. But, if one day, my father is in Hindu Heaven, in Swarga Loka, I think I would want to also be in Hindu Heaven to see him. If only one of them exists, then I don't think I want that Heaven either way. I want Heaven to be with both of them. Otherwise, it wouldn't be Heaven."

"It is up to us to have faith that Heaven exists," said Aunt Vidya. "That is all."

"But what Heaven do I turn to? If I want to see my parents in Heaven, I am forced to disbelieve one of them, to admit that one must be wrong. Otherwise, I must make my own Heaven which means both of them are wrong."

Aunt Vidya paused for a moment and seemed to be thinking very deeply. She stepped towards me and sat on the chair next to me again.

"I know where you get your curiosity from, Dhaval. You get it from your mother. She was brilliant too, always reading, always learning. And not a day goes by that we all don't miss her dearly. And I believe she would have had a better answer for you than me. I cannot tell you exactly what Heaven is because I have never seen it. All I can tell you is that I believe in a Heaven where our loved ones will be with us one day, and we will be delighted. And you may call that Heaven Swarga Loka or you may call it simply Heaven without any better name, but it is a place where I believe we will one day be. Whatever you decide doesn't change what Heaven is. Heaven is already Heaven. For me and indeed, for your father, that is Swarga Loka. But you cannot create what has already been created. All you can do is try to imagine the glory of what Heaven would be. I think we go to another place of infinite love," she replied. "I believe Heaven is a place where we are all together, where everything you've ever dreamt and hoped comes true."

# CHAPTER 15 FERAL

People often forget about the smell, which is strange because it's the sense most connected to memory. We become so interested in sight and sound, maverick visual artists, and rock star lead singers, but who knows the name of a master perfumer? Why don't we think of smell? Smells can put us to sleep and wake us up. A single fragrance can take us back to a place much more instantly and powerfully than any photograph or audio recording. It's why ex-lovers try so hard to keep an article of their once-over's clothing, to feel that feeling again as if they were in the room. It's the smell that often binds lovers. It's the smell that often attunes our senses to a threat. When I think of smell now, I think of the places it brings me back to where I feel scared or lonely.

A few raindrops hit the glass window.

It was the month of June again as monsoon clouds covered the skies and the sea roared for the overflowing rivers. Father was preparing for another business trip. The monsoon rains deepened as continuous pellets of rain hit the window, creating an accidental melody on the glass. I could see it stretched before me, the luminescent rice paddies, the coconut and areca nut groves, and the glowing green grass draping the banks of the two rivers of Mangalore, Netravati, and Gurupura, that flowed on either side of Paradise, framing the landscape.

Both rivers originate at the tip of the Western Ghats, some 1500 meters above the plateau level of Paradise, more than a hundred kilometers away in the thick forest valley. Both ultimately flow into the Arabian Sea. During the monsoon, when the sky turns dark grey, and a torrential downpour hits the land, these two rivers swell like wild beasts, dangerous and unpredictable, often doubling or tripling in size, as streams and canals become surges and trickles become torrents, inundating the paddy fields.

I felt feral, unable to play in the rain as I saw children play puddle jumping, experimenting with floating and sinking with different items, and playing puddle music. I wasn't allowed to go anywhere. I was rarely allowed to leave the house or stray too far. The surrounding jungle only seemed to taunt me. Each hollering of a monkey, each call of a bird, every time the rains came and released their scent from the soil, I became numb to it. Somewhere inside myself, I was still in those whitewashed walls of the hospital, and I was emotionless.

I had no friends, barely anyone to talk to. I was educated till primary at home. My father was extremely strict about my studies, and my home tutors were instructed not to waste any time. If I were even seen as "slacking off," I would be instantly reprimanded. In everything my tutors told me, I would hear my father. "Straighten up! Chin up! Shoulder back!", "Study hard, and you'll achieve something!" They would say, and I knew these were my father's exact words.

All the while, when I was alone in my bed at night watching the stars through my window, I secretly worried that it was because my parents called me Dave that the Gods were angry and had punished me with such torment. What mortal dares to be called a God? Or even pure?

"Aunt Vidya, why me?" I often asked her when she massaged my head on the terrace in the mornings.

Aunt Vidya smiled, and she was always smiling. She faced the sky, clapped her hands, and said, "Dhaval, you are to change the world!"

In the intervals between my home lessons, I would wander like a caged tiger up and down the hallways, trying to appease my restless mind. And every day, I would sit on the front terrace and look out upon the world. Sometimes I thought of running away from the house, running into the jungle, and taking my chances with the tigers and the snakes. I daydreamed about becoming a jungle boy, eating only from fruit trees I would find in the jungle; mangoes, mangosteens, jackfruit, hog plums, or perhaps becoming a laborer, starting a new life as a new kid. I would call myself Deepak Singh, create a jungle fortress and make a whole new world where no child would ever be told what to do.

# CHAPTER 16 REALITY

I would watch with interest the laborers working their tractors to plow the fields, till the soil, irrigate the fields, shovel hay, pile hay onto the tractors, work on the paddy fields, harvest crops of paddy, pulses, coconut, areca nut, and fishing, all the while making my father wealthier every year. And in the evening, I watched them fetch water from the river, wash their clothes, and cook their meals for supper.

For a long time, I thought and tried to feel something other than the numbness I knew had consumed my father.

But oh, was I bored! How many nights have I stayed awake with my active mind going insane? I couldn't do anything or go anywhere because I wasn't allowed because of my condition. I would stare at every square pixel of my room. I would watch every shadow. I would dream every dream. And then I would do it all again. My life was drudgery—everything cyclic. There was nothing new. To me, that was already a form of death.

Being so bored, I snuck into my mother's old room. Father had left everything as if she could turn up any day. Not a single surface had been dusted in weeks, and nothing had been shifted since the day mother must have run into that room when she forgot her handbag before she got back into that car.

The scent of cedar, dust, and leather emanated in the room. By the large window, there was a large rosewood desk with ornate drawers and trays that pulled out from the sides so you could put paper or stationary on them. On top of the desk were many books, long gathering dust, and a little inkwell with a small collection of fountain pens. Dust floated innocently through the air. A soft light streamed through the window.

I loved books. I always had. I loved them for so many reasons, not only because of the stories and information they contained but the smell of books, the feel of books, the variety of books, and the essence of books. But somehow and for some reason, after my mother's death, I would sit there in that study, on my small wooden chair in front of a wall of books, and stare at them. I didn't want to read anymore because, somehow, reading reminded me of my mother's voice, as if all literature was to be read in her exact accent and her same lilt, which I knew all too well. I would sit there, watching dust and looking at books neatly stacked on shelves. They were also sitting and watching me, I suppose, gathering and watching dust. And all the while, I imagined all words in those many books entering my mind somehow as if through osmosis. I imagined knowledge seeping into my brain.

I traced my fingers along the spines of the books, and in the corner of the bookshelf, I found a large wooden box. I pulled it from the shelf and opened it to find a small stack of vinyl records. I looked at each one with curiosity.

I would play them on the record player on low volume because my father would get angry if he heard any noise. And I would listen to everything, like every single sound. The thing about records was that it was always different.

Whenever I'd hear a song, whether it was Van Morrison, the Stranglers, or Elvis Costello, I'd listen and feel calm for once. I would listen to how the melody moved up and down, and I knew these people were adults and belonged to a world I didn't yet truly inhabit, but I knew they understood something I was looking for. They represented a direction. But I was a farm boy with a brain condition, not living in an old time, but I may as well have been. I was growing up in the 90s, but I may as well have been growing up fifty years before. I had no idea of the pop culture world.

Suddenly, I heard a lot of shouting from the other end of the house. I left mother's old room, covering my tracks in the dust, and slipped into the hallway like a fox. I could hear some commotion downstairs.

There had been an accident on the estate; a tractor worker had been injured. His head was bleeding. His skin was pale. And I knew that he was going to die.

I heard many men and women running and shouting. They were bloodied too. I stopped and hid my head behind the wall. I felt the heat of tears flowing down my cheeks. I didn't cry or move, but I felt the entire world was wrong.

I returned to the room, collected the vinyl LPS, put them on the record player, and played them with headphones on to drown out all the other noise. As I was listening, I opened a box underneath the table; it contained a few old photographs, primarily random images of nature, a field of grass, a cityscape, and a photo of my mother laughing at the dinner table with a glass of white wine in her hand, and a couple of books covered in dust. Plus, some books, some paperbacks of classic literature: The Count of Monte Cristo, Dostoevsky, Tolstoy, The Hunchback of Notre Dame, a book by John Keats, Dylan Thomas, and a leather-bound journal which I opened to see my mother's handwriting and lines of poetry. The ink of the letters gleamed, all smooth and lustrous. In the box, I also found half of a polaroid photo revealing my father dancing. It was an image of my father I had almost forgotten, an image of him being happy. Right at the bottom of the cardboard box was a photo of what I guessed was my mother's hometown back in California. It was a photo of my mother when she must have been still a teenager, standing in the dunes on the beach, wearing a straw hat, in a pink and white striped bathing suit, holding onto her hat, so it didn't blow away and smiling. I flipped over the creased photo to see a message written in black pen, in cursive, old-fashioned writing, the way people still wrote in the 1960s before computer keyboards corrupted our hands:

Go all the way.

# CHAPTER 17 SIMPLICITY

In all that time, what I craved most was simplicity. Like a mad scientist in the middle of some grand experiment, I wanted the entire world to leave me alone.

Like a potter's wheel, my mind continued to turn, to spin through my reasoning, the justification for my separation from the world. I was still young and damp clay, but I felt like a potter's creation dancing into form.

All the time, my father had nothing to do with me. He communicated with me through my Aunt Vidya. And this made me feel isolated from him. I wanted to be everything he wasn't, and I felt bitter against him.

I could already sense that he was unlike me at that age. He rejected simplicity. While I had long questioned why things were built and why anyone was ever forced to go to school, work, follow conventions and rules, and get trapped into illusions, it occurred to me that my father was well following those mechanisms. He was the one building new things, new residential buildings, new hotels, new shopping malls, and new hospitals. He entertained other business and political minds to win their cooperation to create a business nexus. He was part of the reason so many were shut out. Yes, he made a lot of money and was respected for this, but why? I asked myself. He never seemed to give a single cent back to anyone. If he built a hospital, he would consider health a money-making industry.

I had watched my father's business workings with a tremendous interest for so long, but now I looked at his work as a joke. Gradually, it seemed his business was simply something that entrapped him, made him bitter and unpleasant, progressively melancholic. I vowed to avoid a business because I saw my father's business as taking him away from me. But beyond this, it seemed to me that my father had been caught in that world for too long, that he had given into avarice which had been a shackle around his feet.

I had never witnessed him smile, never seen him laugh, and never seen him feel any happiness since mother had died. And I think he blamed me for what had happened.

He now did everything possible to keep me away from his world. Every day he would get drunk. Every day he would yell and shout. And every day, I would slip away into daydreams and fantasies to escape from his world. He wanted me to be like him. He wanted me to have status and wealthy friends. But I wanted to be with low-caste children, playing with them. I wanted a better life for all workers at Paradise. He wanted me to understand the importance of money and to have a position where it didn't matter if you treated people disrespectfully because you had enough power. He changed. He was a different person when my mother was around. Now he was cold, ruthless even.

I lost count of the days that passed. I had no concept of time. I guess greed for wealth, power, and status has no end once we start craving, and that was what exactly happened with my dad. Day in and day out, he was only thinking about expanding businesses, meeting business and political people, inking new deals, and thinking about more money, power, and status. In doing so, he forgot about relationships, forgot about me, forgot about humanity, and most importantly, forgot to live a good and relaxed life. But I could think only of one thing: getting away from him.

# CHAPTER 18
# EXPLANATIONS

The years went by. My father did the only thing he could think of. He concentrated on his work. At that time, he was in the middle of a deal to buy a big hotel somewhere in Mumbai, the financial capital of India. The place where he now lived most of the time. He said he wanted me to have a professional education, and he would teach me all he knew about the hotel business. Nowadays, he visits Paradise only during big festivals, and as usual, he left me with my Aunt Vidya to help me with my studies. But I was also supported by many hired tutors to learn the way of the world to become a gentleman.

I loved Aunt Vidya. We had similar attitudes. She had always been with me forever, and I did love her. But I had come to think of myself as different from my father. And as this thought grew in my mind, I began to despise even those I felt closest to. I was full of doubts. What had he done to me? Why had he left me like this? What was I doing? I was so lost. I was drowning in doubt. I didn't trust anyone. I didn't trust myself. I didn't trust my father. I didn't trust anything anymore. Only nature relieved me of the chaos. It was only natural that it was always there for me, and I kept my doors open.

Since my father was away most of the time, Aunt Vidya allowed me to play with poor low-caste children, though I was constantly watched for my safety. Though they hardly spoke English as they went to local public schools, studying in the Kannada language, it didn't affect our good times playing barefoot in the empty paddy fields with mud and stones. This helped me to connect with nature. I learned their Tulu and Kannada languages in bits and pieces, and they picked up some English words from me. This relieved my loneliness to a certain extent.

Eventually, I went to boarding school for my high school studies in Mangalore. I still lived with my father when he was in town, but Aunt Vidya helped me when I was in trouble. She was my whole world. So was my mother, I thought, but then I didn't think of her very often, either. She was always swamped too, and we drifted apart. She taught me to trust myself and believe in my life, but I was again spinning through a new reality.

In school, I was a loner. I talked to no one and interacted with no one unless I had to. I fell asleep often in class, but I was the one student who had a pardon for that because of my condition. The other children were told not to taunt me, but they did. Though I didn't care. I didn't want to know them. They seemed of another world I didn't belong to. They talked of the latest popular music, Indian cricketers, Bollywood movies, and celebrities; I knew nothing. It seemed I was completely living in another era. And because the students were told explicitly not to mock me, also a result of my father being held in high regard by the school for donating a large sum of money to their science wing, and because the teachers were told not to scold me for falling asleep, I became like a ghost in school, often falling asleep on purpose or pretending to fall asleep just because I wanted to escape the repressing thing called school.

My life had become a void, a black hole of uncertainty, and I felt dead.

At this stage, I had only one thing to live for: finish high school and get into college. I had one thing to complete my life, one goal, which wasn't even mine. It was my father's. He insisted I "make something of my life," which meant either becoming a doctor to run his hospitals or a businessman to run his new luxury hotel business. Because of my condition, it was thought that a brain surgeon who could fall asleep during the surgery might not be the best option. Then, as I was perceived to be good with words and often read, the next option was an intelligent business degree.

The family doctor, or the equivalent of a family doctor in India, came to the house long weekends to check my brain condition. I had a great desire to understand life, a desire I would not have until many years later. I wanted to find answers. So, I would talk to him. He seemed to be a good listener. And often, all he did was listen, nod, and shake his head as I explained what it felt like when I fell asleep. I remember him saying "Yes, yes" a lot. He would nod his head up and down a lot, poke his little light in my ears, or flash it in my eyes. Aunt Vidya often asked him to use her medicinal remedies, but he would scoff, saying it was all voodoo.

"What happens when you lose consciousness?" he asked.

"I see shapes," I replied.

"What kinds of shapes?"

"Complex geometrical patterns, and I see colors and all kinds of amazing things. I don't lose consciousness really at all. If anything, I fall awake in that world."

Aunt Vidya liked to think I should become a priest, for she had always felt that I was connected to something divine, but the doctor insisted my visions were purely psychological. And my father insisted business degree was the best option for me because it would grant me a place in society in my new world. And because, as he would say, I was good at reading people and understanding their subtle, psychological aspects.

A few boys at school already had girlfriends, and I overheard them talking, explaining what they, in turn, had overheard, that without a girlfriend, one would be called a "dumb boy." The boys and girls talked and held hands in secret and laughed their hearts out. What is it like having a girlfriend and talking to them? Was I at a disadvantage by getting home-schooled in primary because of my condition? These questions troubled me. Everywhere I turned, there seemed to be people giving me their opinions on things, and not only that, forcing those opinions on me. I was probably the most unpopular in the whole school, as much as I was the most independent, for everyone hated me for it.

When I came home on long weekends, I had clarity in my learning in my conversations with nature, and I felt more independent than ever. I went out playing with boys and looked for every opportunity to gain the experience of talking to girls who were always put up at home to carry out household works when parents worked in the fields. I thought this would help me have a girlfriend at the school to shed my 'dumb boy' title.

# CHAPTER 19 DIWALI

Chow pow shrreeeeee.

The firecrackers blazed across the sky.

It was late October, and all of India celebrated Diwali, the festival of lights dedicated to Goddess Laxmi. This year, Paradise celebrated a special Diwali at the beginning of the new millennium. I was sixteen at the time, but I was always happy to escape back home for the five-day holidays from the boarding school. A tika, a vertical rainbow of protective smudges, was painted on my forehead. This was the festival's final day, Bhai tika, on which brothers and sisters blessed each other.

My father's mansion glowed on the top of the hill. The forecourt of the villa was decorated with colorful fabrics, and the garden pathways were lined with white and yellow roses. Everywhere was decorated with billions of sparkling days, which you might call oil lamps. Sisters blessed their brothers, and brothers gave gifts to their sisters.

The beats of drums reverberated. Children fired crackers into the sky that continued to pop in glittering green, blue, and pink.

The fires flickered their light on all our faces as hundreds of villagers gathered in a circle. Some young girls danced in the center of a process in a clearing not far from the river, down the hill. The laborers and their families danced and sang traditional folk songs. Boys and girls, young and the elderly, all danced. The colony buzzed from the children running amid the crowd.

Everyone smiled as they saw me. Some of the older people had joined their children in dancing around the bonfire; they seemed to me to move like vines creeping into the sun. Every movement seemed so natural, for they were feeling every note of the melodies in their souls, not thinking about the dance movements. They were feeling and letting their bodies react like sea anemones in a storm pushed by the currents of the water. They couldn't help but dance.

All around, people were chattering and laughing and singing. It's funny how life plays these tricks on you. When you let down your guard, and you think you're all alone in the world, when you feel you are separate for a moment from the world, how you are free from the tangents of life, free from the tangled story of your adventure, suddenly the universe finds some way to pull you back into the vortex, to throw you off balance, sometimes in the most beautiful way. At that moment, looking at the sky, for a moment, I felt I saw the white clouds, like dragon scales, transposed upon the colors of it. That's when I saw her.

Suddenly I was snapped out of my revelry by a man offering me a betel leaf. Thc tradition of eating paan with soaked lime and areca nut (supari) with tobacco is age-old. Betel is also used in religious rituals, festivals, and prayers as it is considered auspicious. But when I looked back to see where the girl was, I noticed she was gone, no longer dancing around the fire. I only saw a crowd of unknown people for a moment, just like tree leaves had unveiled her image in the jungle before. I was mesmerized by her flowing hair as if she had fallen out of a Botticelli painting.

I thought she was the most beautiful woman I'd ever seen. I was sure of it. I saw the curtain of the crowd around her step back, and there she was! The beautiful young woman, wearing a moss and yellow churidar.

I supposed she was the same girl who disappeared in the jungle as I hadn't recognized her, for she looked suddenly grown up, no longer a girl but a young woman. It had been so long since I'd seen her. She looked like a nymph; I thought – something I had only seen in Greek or Roman mythology books. You might even say she was pretty thin but with wide hips that seemed borrowed from another slightly wider body. Her hair caught the golden sunlight, swiveled in locks, and her skin glowed like porcelain. Looking at her, I felt time slow down as adrenaline shot through my veins. Yes, if she was a nymph, I was a satyr. I knew at that moment that I wanted her. I tried to leap at her from out of the trees, sit her down by the side of a river, and play for her the ancient melodies of the Gods on his wooden flute while dancing my hooves into the dirt.

For a moment, I didn't know what to say. I was in a Botticelli painting, seeing her turquoise dress. Her hair was loose around her shoulders, her eyes soft and alive. Her lips were peach red. That smile. She belonged to another world, I thought. She was made to float on giant seashells, be showered by roses, and be surrounded by angels.

# CHAPTER 20 DANCING

I wasn't used to having all the pieces of myself falling into place. I knew I wanted to dance with her. I wanted to ask her to be by my side. As far as I was concerned, she was the one. I was sure of it. In every fiber of my body. But how? It wasn't a simple question. I knew I wanted to be closer to her, that was all.

Then she turned my way and said, "Dhaval?"

And yet, at that moment, I didn't say anything, and I just stood there like a deer seeing the headlights. She looked at me with a curious look on her face, her hand fidgeting with the strap of her bag before she smiled warmly.

“My name …… Asha, Come dance?” she asked in her broken English.

"Well, look, the thing is, I'm—"

"Don’t know… how…..dance?"

"Well, yes, I know some dance. My mother wasn't from India. She taught me the—"

"Taught you…… what?"

"I grew up listening to Van Morrison, Joe Cocker, Elvis—"

"Elvis!" Asha laughed. "Come," she said again. "I .... teach you. Not difficult...... you must .....move.... your... body.... Simple."

That night, I danced as I had never danced before. The very truth was I hadn't. Still, I danced like I didn't think anyone had ever danced. I don't know if it was the paan or whatever was in that betel leaf, but I felt somehow like I had shed my old self. I felt free. I felt electric. I felt like I was dying and coming to life all at once as I had just been given a second chance, as I had constantly been feeling before I knew how to explain it. Before I knew it, I was caught up in the circle. I tried to dance as the drumming of the festival reached a syncopated rhythm, and I felt it moving through every part of my body.

All around us, a hundred people danced Indian style as Asha and I danced. The celebration around us was becoming rowdier. The surrounding crowd chanted, counting down. I looked down at my feet, moving out of time. I had two left feet.

"... Five!"

But Asha moved with me and guided me while we danced a kind of waltz, half Bollywood, half Elvis rock.

"... Four!"

I felt myself leaning into Asha.

"... Three!"

For a moment, I thought of kissing her.

"... Two!"

The drums hit their crescendos.

"... One!"

Fireworks burst. People cheered.

Suddenly I noticed the group was looking at me with Asha. A brahmin dancing with a lower caste. I felt their eyes hot on my back. I saw the crowd scatter, and I looked up the hill to see a figure on the mountain near the mansion. The group turned their attention to the fireworks above. Asha stepped back with me from the circle. She turned to me, seeing I was giddy and gripping my head in pain, and she pulled me away from the group.

"What's wrong?" asked Asha.

"It must be the lights; I think I'm going to faint."

"Then you must be more like Krishna than you thought," said Asha, and for a moment, the Festival of Lights appeared as a kind of battlefield on which Krishna had fainted. "Come on," she said.

"Where are we going?" I asked.

She turned back to me, her eyes wide, a massive grin on her face, "Who knows!"

# CHAPTER 21 LOVE HEART TREE

The bonfires of the festivities faded behind us though their lights still streaked across the face of the sky as we walked back through the coconut and areca nut trees up to the cliffs that overlooked the paddy fields. There were thick clusters of trees on the outskirts of the upper tier on which the mansion was built. There were two particular trees in this cluster that, unlike the others on our property, leaned into rather than away from each other. Their canopies were covered in such a way as to make a heart shape of their plume of leaves. These two entangled trees offered a kind of seat high above the world. These trees looked like two lovers leaning into one another, like Ginger Baker and Fred Astaire, eternally dancing.

I called it the love-heart tree.

Before I could think of a good excuse not to climb the tree, Asha was already hoisting herself up on the lowest branch, gaining a foothold and then pulling herself up again, lifting herself branch by branch, though a yellow sash of fabric ripped and now hung from a splintered branch. But she continued, pushing through the veil of vines until finally, I could see her face but a couple of meters away as she lifted herself into the tree's heart before looking back down at me.

"What are you waiting for?" she beckoned.

"I ... I ..." I didn't know how to explain that I had never climbed a tree before. Mother said it was not wise to climb anything you could feasibly fall out, including chairs, bar stools, or a chest of drawers.

"Come up!"

Lower branches branched out from the tree trunk, and grabbing hold of one, I hoisted myself up to the lower level upon the box. Grabbing hold of another branch higher above my head, I lifted myself into the base fork of the tree, and from there, I again grappled onto yet another branch, lifting myself. Again and again, I found a foothold and lifted myself ever higher till I found myself in the heart of where the two trees crossed.

That night we found ourselves beneath the stars and suspended above the entire world. From that vantage, we could see the bonfires of the party still raging, the party continuing without us.

And there she was, her face red and hair concerned with bits of bark, Asha. But in the drizzle, she appeared to shine. She found space on the broad branch near me and sat to find her breath again. In that moment of silence, she too seemed to go quiet as if hypnotized by the beauty around us as she, for the first time, took in the view of the yellow fields and the distant coconut trees in the pink and purple sunset lit up by red, orange, blue and yellow bonfire flame.

We sat there for what felt like a good few minutes, neither of us saying a word, seemingly mesmerized, overlooking Paradise. From that vantage, the whole world opened up to me in splendor. I could see the whole of Paradise Island, the sweeping valley, the lush, yellow paddy fields, our mansion, the large coconut trees, the colorful plants of our garden, and the distant jungle glowed up by billions of Diwali lights, Diyas against the splendor of sunset. I could see everything! I tucked my body in between the colorful branches of the tree and sighted myriad butterflies fluttering up through the ascending vines.

# CHAPTER 22 INTERACTION

It seemed the whole world, like a dazzling vortex, had thrown itself suddenly at my eyes no different than a lover throwing themselves at their long lost love. It felt euphoric, like nothing I'd ever felt before. And on leaving me back in reality again, I felt like the abandoned child left to drift in the stream once more, destined for whatever fate or rocks or reeds would welcome me. Butterflies swarmed once more as if chased by something unseen, and suddenly, the colors of the natural world returned to my eyes. It was darker now, the first patches of purple-pink flooding the sunset sky.

The rustling of the leaves seemed to sing its song, and for a moment, I was sure that warmth was again flooding into the delta of my heart as my eyelids grew heavy and the entire world seemed to slow. Fearing I might fall off the tree, I hooked my foot into the crook of the branch where the two trees intertwined and wrapped my arm around some dangling vines. And as if the scent of the vines and the ylang-ylang were an elixir of incense, black, colorless patches drifted upon my eyes. It was all too perfect, almost as if the place was paradise. But then, suddenly, the world started to blur and shift around me, and I thought I would faint.

"Where do you?" asked Asha.

"What do you mean?" I replied.

"Sometimes you are here; sometimes you seem somewhere else in another world. My mum said people like you live in two worlds," Asha said in a mix of Tulu and broken English.

"What two worlds would they be?"

"The world of wakefulness and the world of sleep."

" I was in a car accident when I was very young; that's when it started. I don't remember ever experiencing it before."

"Do you remember the accident?"

"Of course, I will never forget it. I am seeing the world upside down like that. Everything spinning. That's how I feel most of the time, like my head is spinning. It isn't easy to get a hold of it. Part of me is still in that car, flipped upside down. It was like a dream."

"Ah, but what is a dream?" She asked. "Once, I dreamt that I was a butterfly; when I woke up, I did not know whether I was the man dreaming he was a butterfly or the butterfly dreaming he was a man. The reality we think is not always the true reality. What we think is the dream might be wakefulness; what we think is waking life might very well be the dream."

We sat there in silence, watching the bonfires, before Asha continued, "I heard that you read all the time. What is it in those books that fascinate you so much?" she asked.

"I like stories," I replied. "My mother used to tell stories to me all the time."

"Don't you have a story?" she asked.

"I guess I've never thought about it before."

"Tell me one."

I stared into the distance for a moment. "What if I told you a story that's never been told?"

"I would say tell it."

"What if I also told you that by telling you this story, you will never forget it? For all your life, you will carry it with you. It will be so beautiful and bold that it will sit with you like in your pocket and change you because it cannot help change you."

"I would still say tell it."

"What if I also told you the beauty of the story is so grand that it is at first unfathomable, and you won't realize how much the story is changing your life until never."

"I would still say tell it."

"What if I told you the story will never end, and you will not know when it will end?"

"It sounds like a pretty bad story. Now I'm thinking, don't tell it."

"Very well then, I will tell you the story."

"Tell it then ..."

"I don't know where to start," I said.

"Then how does the story end?" asked Asha.

"I don't know," I replied.

"What do you mean you don't know?"

"I told you the nature of the story; you still wanted to hear it."

"It needs an ending," replied Asha.

Then we looked at each other in silence. The distant river shone like cellophane. The scent of the flowers had already enveloped us in its magic spell. I felt that in her eyes, I could see the true depths of the universe. I could see the start and end of all things, that everything constantly revolves. Looking through the dark tunnels of her pupils, I thought that perhaps, just perhaps, I could see her soul.

# CHAPTER 23 DESIRE

I knew I wanted to know more about her life, caste, favorite color, everything. I wanted to learn more about her than I knew about my right hand. I wanted to know her like I wanted to see each star in the sky, what it was, where each speck of light came from, and where each bit of light would go. And just as all the stars in the universe are just the consequence of an explosion, little specks of that grand firework of existence born from the point of singularity as Asha herself had told me, I saw in her that same explosion of matter and soul. I saw the fusion of stars and the tearing of supernovas. And in those moments, I was convinced I was dreaming, that I had fallen asleep, that I was still lying in the turmeric plants somewhere back in the younger years of my childhood.

Looking into the distance, I marveled at the jigsaw puzzle fields and a few random birds flying over a scattering of darkness. The world started to dimmer, and I felt like I was falling asleep. Falling Fireworks lit up the sky, their embers glowing and falling like rain in the form of sequins. That drumming again filled my head and filled my mind. I felt myself falling into a gorge. "Not now ... Not now," I again said to myself.

And as dusk fell, a soft rain began to fall, and we found ourselves in the shadows of a nearby cluster of trees. As I stared into her eyes, I knew. Finally, I knew she was the one. It all happened so gently, so effortlessly, and I don't even remember whether I leaned in first or her. Just as Asha placed her head in her hands, her lips were on mine, my lips were on hers, and my hands were on her hips. We kissed beneath a coconut tree, with her back against the trunk of it and me leaning into her. I felt an eternity in that kiss as the pink sunset threw flickered patterns of light upon our faces, the bonfire of the celebrations raged, and the light flickered through as purple and pink and blue as the fireworks beneath my closed eyelids.

I opened my eyes to see if I was still sitting on that same branch, my arms still tangled in vines, my foot still awkwardly stuck in the crook of the two units, surrounded by nature's parasol of leaves. I did not know how long I had been in my trance watching the fireworks.

It was as if a giant bonfire had been lit in my soul, and we had become one flame. As the faint light of bonfires started to fade into the dark of night, we hugged and kissed, and all the many worlds that ever existed in the universe seemed to me then to stop. At the same time, everything suddenly felt in fast motion.

What was this new feeling? This sensation of surging energy throughout my entire being as if I were surfing a wave of the entire world? I did not know what to do with it. I did not know where I wanted it to go or where it came from! I just knew I wanted her. I wanted her body, her mind; I wanted her soul. I wanted not just to be against her, skin against skin, but to be fused with her, for it felt that that would be the only way I would ever be complete again. As if I was only ever half of something divine without her. But with her! I became my whole self! Ah! The love of a man for a woman! The love of a woman for a man! The most potent energy known to us is the energy of opposites pushing and pulling. It is the cosmic force that we call the divine! It is love! It is the glory of creation!

We stayed in that tree that night for what felt like years, but it was probably more like an hour. We held each other, entwined in a passion and a love far beyond the physical. It was as if our very souls had been fused, and I never wanted to be broken away from her again.

I felt my blood heating up. I saw her eyes, full of stars and moonlight.

The last rays of sunset shone upon the land. The shrubs that covered the entire hill and the bloomed, little, white flowers seemed to glow as they caught the last of the day's light, making the hillside appear speckled as if it were covered in snow. And we stood beneath the love-heart tree. Asha turned her attention back to the tree branch; I thought the bark must have enchanted her for a moment before I noticed her holding a sliver of silk.

She tied the silk around the tree.

"I see," replied Asha. "That is a long way away; I hope you will visit from time to time."

"Well, that's the thing, Asha. When will I see you again? What if I don't want to visit sometimes?"

"Promise," she said. "We will meet back here at this tree if we are parted. We promise that we will love each other. And if the love is strong enough, we will return here. We will tie a yellow ribbon around this tree and know that the other has arrived and that we will meet here again."

"I promise," I said.

# CHAPTER 24 DILIGENCE

Most boys, when they hit their growth spurts, needed new clothes. Shirts with collars and ties. Denim that was a shade or two too tight. Sturdy shoes. Dresses. Jeans. Shirts.

When I went back to my boarding to complete my years 11 and 12, I had a sudden energy, a will; I didn't know why. I decided I would read more, write more, and explore more. I decided if I was to be a loner, I might as well be an educated intellectual, perhaps even an academic loner. I read voraciously. Every day I read in the school library. I read books that most teens at that age didn't even know existed—the works of Shakespeare, and Plato, religious texts like the Bible, Quran, and the Vedas. I often read multiple books at a time, juggling complex ideas from each book and building bridges of analogies in my mind. More and more, I became fascinated with the world through this portal and lens of words. But there was something more to this endeavor too. I read not just for entertainment but to find answers. I dedicated myself to finding the solution I indeed sought after. The question of what was the dream and was the real world. Before I knew it, I was on this quest for enlightenment.

My boarding bed was a study in detachment. Papers, crumpled and half-finished, were piled on a bedside table. Books rolled and clutched in stacks lay piled in and around the top and sides of the bed. My curiosity for the world was growing more profound, and I would let nothing stand in the way. This was the way I could find the answers. This was where I could find the real world, where I had lived my whole life but had never seen it. I would sit there in the dark and let the world wash over me.

I read about Plato's cave, Krishnamurti, Osho, and Shakespeare's tragedies. And to be honest, many of these books were still beyond me in intellectual scope. I was still young. But I was also tenacious. My passion for learning was an eternal fire. And for all the strange and mysterious remedies my Aunt Vidya had given me, it seemed I had found the solution that worked the best so far: my own will and passion in the form of focus. Though I could not talk to my father about such things, I could confide in Aunt Vidya. She had taught me the basics of meditation and even mantras. Inspired by her and these books on reflection, I started meditating for hours. I would try to collect my thoughts and will myself into the place of dreams I was forced into many times due to my broken brain. I forced myself into the dark recesses of my mind.

And then, one day, Aunt Vidya came to see me. She was happy to see me much better than I had been a few months back. She saw I had found a new passion for learning and reading, and she was happy for me. My brain condition seemed better now, not so disruptive in my life. We went to the nearby coffee shop; she made me sit down and explained that she was leaving because she needed to return to her divine calling to be a hermit in northern India. I was heartbroken. She had taught me about the world and even seemed to give me insight into the spiritual world. What will happen to me now? I thought. I would be on my own.

"You are growing older, Dhaval, and there is no reason for me to stay here anymore. I have taught you so much. And I know it's been many years. Remember, you will always be special to me, and I know I will be special to you. Now onwards, the best thing I can do for you is to pray for you, but I must go."

I remember standing in front of the hostel gate, tears streaming down my face, waving to her as she left. But she was right; I was older now. And I was ready to live my life, and I was prepared to become a man.

# CHAPTER 25 REVELATION

The love-heart tree had changed very little over the years. From that vantage on that snow-petal hill, the new world now opened up once more to me. The slopes were again covered in white petals that looked like snow. The landscape of coconut trees, paddy fields, and the jungle around seemed to dance on the snaking rivers, with the beats of streams bubbling over rocks and branches as the myriad of birds fluttered through the cascading branches from the subtle breeze.

I stood before the tree and tied a yellow ribbon around the trunk. At that moment, I was hit by a kind of mini epiphany. I felt the hairs stand up on the back of my neck. I had stopped and was staring into a patch of trees in a daze. I couldn't put my finger on it, but I felt as if something big was about to happen, like a storm was about to hit, the kind of electrical charge you feel when the hairs on your neck stand on end. But the sky was clear.

I felt something I had not felt in a long time. A feeling I couldn't quite describe. It was pulling in my stomach—an emptiness. Something like regret, though different, for I felt suddenly absorbed by an overwhelming sense of nostalgia as though I had been hit by a sudden warm breeze belonging to another time and place. I felt as if I were being pulled back by an invisible string.

She appeared to shine like a diamond in the bright sunshine passing through the thick branches and leaves. I couldn't understand what made her look so beautiful then, and I wasn't entirely sure. It was as if some halo of light emanated from around her. Something glowed within her so fiercely and so beautiful that I feared I could never bear to look at anything else but her again. Her hair flowed gently around her shoulders.

"It is beautiful here, isn't it?" I said.

"That's why I come up here," Asha replied. "It's a nice place to hide and enjoy the music of the butterflies."

I laughed. "Ha! Asha, you are a natural comedian! Butterflies don't play music!"

"Sure they do," she replied, her gentleness returning now that she had caught her breath again after the climb. "You have to listen. You'd be surprised what things make music. Flowers, for example. Listening to a flower very closely might take a day or two, but eventually, you will hear the blossoming new fronds and shoots singing. It's just different from normal sound. But they sing. I swear they sing!"

"You're a unique person," I told Asha.

"My mother was right; you're a dreamer," she replied.

I couldn't help but smile now as I felt like a man looking into the face of the sun, like Icarus about to burst into flames. I had never felt such an instant dose of endorphin flood my brain. For so long, the truth was that I had suffered from an affliction that was perhaps sometimes more debilitating than any physical disability. All my senses worked fine, my eyesight was 20/20, and if I closed my eyes, I could hear a pin drop onto the floor, but for so long, I had felt a constant numbness – a feeling that nothing mattered anymore. The visuals that were fed through my optic nerve no longer appeared dull. Scent no longer turned my head. Food lacked taste. I had suffered from a gradually worsening feeling that I had seen, heard, felt, and even tasted. Yet, as I described these images to Asha, I felt everything coming alive again, that everything suddenly mattered. No matter how small. The world seemed brighter, perhaps even tastier, filled with a bizarre majesty I had never felt before. And all of a sudden, it hit me. Like a stupid fool, I'd fallen in love without the first date.

Butterflies swarmed, tempting me into a dream. The tangerine sunset was in swing now, and it would be completely dark with the new moon before long. I knew the nanny would be waiting for me for dinner, and needless to say, father didn't like surprises.

"My father says I am to go to business school," I blurted out.

"Business school?" Asked Asha.

"Yes," I replied. "I cannot escape it. I will be living elsewhere."

Looking at Asha, I suspected she didn't want to return home either. That she, like me, wanted to stay there forever on that branch watching the world drift by. I was very much aware that we were from different castes. But you cannot always help whom you fall in love with, and you don't always have control over how or even why. She was intelligent. She exhibited a depth of knowledge in mathematics, literature, and science. I often wondered how she knew so much, given she was from a low-caste family and studied in public school. It seemed it was only us in existence then—only her and me. And I think I realized then that it was not just an attraction to her that happens to teens, but I was in deep love with her. Not that I knew what this kind of love was or even what to do with it. I just knew that I felt this swarming feeling inside of me, like those ascending butterflies dancing through the vines, a feeling that I'd never really felt before, a feeling that had nowhere to go. The thought of her could only remedy that.

I took a minute to collect myself and was about to say something when Asha bet me to it.

"If you could do anything in the world, what would you do?" asked Asha.

"That's easy," I replied. "I would travel and see the world."

"So, you would study something about world geography or tourism?" she asked.

"No," I replied. "I want to be a writer; I have a distinction in year 12 and a high ranking for admission into a literature course in a competitive exam."

"Then what is holding you back?"

"My father insists I become like him, a businessman."

"Then you must do what he says?"

"What if I don't want to? Don't you ever think about being someone different?"

I rolled over to face Asha on the ground.

"Run away with me," I said.

"What? Why? Where?"

"Somewhere, anywhere, it doesn't matter, just away from here."

"Are you serious?"

"Of course," I replied. "I've never been more serious in my entire life."

"Run away? But Dhaval ..."

"Would it be so complicated?

"Couldn't we do it? I know we are of different castes and backgrounds, but to hell with my father. I do not care about him, Asha. I do not care about his riches. Asha, since that first day I met you in the—"

"Stop," replied Asha, placing her finger on my lips to plug the words. "You need not say any of that."

We kissed.

And I felt my entire world expand as if I were a supernova exploding into complete bliss and unending love. I just wanted to hold her like that forever. Of course, the idea of sex crossed my mind, but I was young, and without knowing the future, even then, I had the maturity to realize I didn't want to put her in a difficult situation. I cared too much for her to do that. So, it seemed that would not happen, so we just lay there, and I smiled, taking in her face, energy, body, smile, voice, and smell. It was intoxicating. More intoxicating than the scent of vanilla!

# CHAPTER 26 REBELLION

When I returned to the house, I ate dinner quietly, went to my room, finished packing my things, and got ready to leave in the morning. Sleep disappeared, and I dreamt of being with Asha from now on as the monsoon rains lashed Paradise.

Early in the morning, I gathered everything. I packed my things in my backpack and took my mother's gold necklace from my father's cupboard drawer.

On leaving, I found father sitting in the small wooden chair by the lounge window.

"I'm leaving," I told him. "I did not expect you to be awake so early, but I must go."

"Now, it is time you complete your university degree so you can return to Paradise and work in the hotel business to make money like me," he said. "If you can't complete the degree, I will find a place for you in the business. You do not have my mind; it is unfortunate. I realize that, but I will find a place for you."

The realization that this was it finally hit me. Now it was here, and I hesitated because I knew exactly why my father had sent Aunt Vidya off. My father can't force his way on me if she was still in Paradise! Because he wanted me to do what he wanted, at least a businessman like him, if not better!

It started as a bit of seed but grew steadily, branches reaching every corner of my psyche. That realization that the time of independence was over. The fear, deep in my stomach, lingered.

His eyes were as dark as night.

"I have spent money to get you into business school," said my father. "I have pulled many strings."

"And did you ever ask me what I wanted?" I replied. "I feel something bigger. I mean, don't you feel something bigger than yourself? Don't you feel something is about to change? There's this nerve of energy in the world like everything is just going to break apart. It's like a runaway locomotive. Whatever happens from here will be massive, don't you feel it? And who knows what it will be, what will become of the world, and what will become of us? But it's going to be amazing! And we're going to be a part of it, and I don't want to be a businessman; I don't want to be part of this system. I want to be part of my system. I want to find my path. Isn't that what you should want of your son? Shouldn't you want me to be happy? I want to help people. I mean, help people on the front lines."

"Dhaval, you know that is not possible."

"Why not?"

"Are you going to live your whole life being foolish, not understanding your name? It is time for you to become like me. To inherit the land and the estate. To take over from my work and develop the business."

"Father, I never wanted to do your work. I've been listening to you; you tell me what to do. And yet, you are never here. I won't do it anymore. I'm leaving."

"And what will you do for work if you have no degree? You'll be an uneducated bum. Is that any life to live?"

"You know what I always hoped for, father? I hoped that one day you and I would sit down and tell me you're proud of me, that you love me, faults and all, and regardless of mother's death, that you don't see her in my eyes anymore. All these years, do you know what I dreamed about? I dreamed that one day, I would graduate from a business school as you wanted me to and that you would be there, and you would say to me, 'Son, I remember the little boy you once were, and I remember giving you the tools to take your first steps toward becoming a man. And I gave you the things you needed to mature in this world. And you've grown, and I am proud to be your father.' Do you understand? All I wanted was to make you proud. I imagined myself and other students receiving their certificates. And as I would step forward and take my certificate, I would scan the crowd of faces, and I would see you there. You, my dad, the same man who had been my teacher and mentor, my dear friend, were standing in the front row of the packed auditorium. I watched as the faces of students lit up. I imagined after graduation, you and I would sit down. I hoped you would tell me you were proud and happy for me that I had done well. But it's all a fantasy. You weren't there before in my life. So why would I expect you to be there from now? And then I realized, why am I even caring about making someone proud who will never be proud of me, a person who will only ever be proud of himself? You weren't there for me, and you were never there."

"Where were you last night?" he asked.

"Father, listen. I can explain," I replied. "I wanted to—"

"You surprise me, Dave. Do you think I don't see what you are doing? Do you think I don't see you outside fraternizing with low-caste girls? You are too much like your mother."

"Father—"

"Listen!" he boomed. "I let you roam outside after your mother's death because I felt sorry for you. She turned you into a weakling. She fashioned you into a boy, not a man, and don't think I didn't see it. For a time, I let it go. Also, because you seemed somehow lonely, you must remember Dave, that you are an heir to Paradise and an Alva! You are not one of that low-caste! They are beneath you, do you understand? You are intent on disgracing me, as you have so far disgraced your family and mother."

"You don't know what she would feel. You're not going to see her anymore! Do you understand?"

"Father, those poor laborers are good people and that girl. She is no different to you or me!"

"You have become rebellious!" said my father. "And now you are in danger of joining those low-caste workers when you grow up! It's our prestige at stake here, don't you understand that? What will they think of us if the other wealthy families see you playing with those young men and women? That we allow such things to happen? That we allow our son to fall down the spiral of self-ruin? That we do not school him properly? What did I do to deserve such disrespect?"

"You demand that everyone listens to you and follows you," I replied. "But people respect you only for your wealth; is that all you want?"

"You are too naive," replied my father. "How you were born, my son, I don't know! You think the low caste people have a place in society, but they do not. And you fall for any woman who blinks at you!"

"But father, I—"

"You are not one of those blacks."

He turned and grabbed me by the cuff of my collar and pushed me up against the wall. "You think I gave you everything all your life for you to turn around and tell me you're going to throw it away! Do you think I'll let you make a fool of the family and me? Of Paradise?"

I met my father's eyes and forced myself not to look away; adrenaline surged through my bones. "I will not fight you."

My father held his fist in front of my face. I was sure he was going to punch me. "I always knew you weren't like me," he said.

"Father, listen. I want your support on this. I am telling you this only because I always want to be truthful and tell you everything. I have been living a lie, father. Everything you've done for me, I understand, I do. But my heart is not in it."

He pushed me, then let me go, stepping back as I slid down the wall in recoil.

"I spent my whole life thinking you were born in the image of me. You are an Alva! Now I realize you are an image of something else."

"I am in love with her, father. And yes, she is a low-caste. She is a Buddhist. Her name is Asha. But I have been in love with her since the first moment I saw her, and I want to be with her, and I know she wants to be with me."

I struck my father, and for a moment, I didn't know what had become of me, holding my fist still before me. I looked at my father and felt pure shame to see him afraid. I pushed him away, backed out of the room, and grabbed my bag. I turned and ran.

# CHAPTER 27 SOUND

I ran out the door, through the garden, past the coconut trees, past the ginger plants, past the snaking river. I ran like a pure jolt of electricity.

As I ran, I heard the onset of the monsoonal rain howling through the air as if it were a truck about to hit me.

The rain pelted my face, and my feet slipped in the mud.

All around me, nature was bent to the force of a growing storm. The coconut trees swayed in the gusting wind and looked like they might snap. The torrent of water surged, cutting its course now through the fields, swamping everything in its path. I couldn't quite make out any visible landmarks. The usual snaking river was no longer its standard shape but now splintered off in a thousand directions, each torrent like a squid tentacle feeling for the sea.

The rain fell like static as I ran along the cliffs, through the trees, and above the beauty of the deep valleys. The chirping of birds and the croaking of frogs fluttered through the air. An empty feeling in my gut continued to swell. Everything hurt. From where I was now, I could see the village from another angle.

I slowed down, almost out of breath, and walked up the dirt path to a lookout over the river. The river was often muddy, and bits of rubbish floated on the sides, especially after a storm. I used to go to the lake as a young child with my parents. I thought of them as I sat over the edge of the barrier overlooking the river. I thought of those blank spaces in the locket.

The sun was veering down, marking strobe-like patterns against the clouds and lighting up the golden purple and pink rocks. The trees waved in the wind on top of the cliff ridge. I breathed in heavily one last time. Yet, at that moment, my lungs were filled with air. I again heard what I could only describe were metal chimes that clung together, making a soft melody in a sudden warm breeze, and a flurry of leaves drifted through the air and then, a sudden tugging at my heart.

A sea of leaves lined the ground, lending their damp, wooden scent to the air. The air seemed damper and cooler again, the leaves wetter, the grass and the trees lusher, the sun muffled by thick clouds.

As I walked further through the park, the crackling of twigs underfoot, the orange haze of the distant city came stringing its way through the remarkable, dark trees, making the air's dust radiate with light and casting mottled shadows across the grass.

Halfway through the trees, running along a dirt path, a flash of white appeared to the side of me. I stopped and turned. The light was moving back and forth as if swaying like a will-o-wisp. A sudden humming started up again. I braced myself, trying to squint into the mist of the darkness. The hairs on my neck stood on end. I looked around me, but all else was dark. That light again appeared as if moving through the trees, but now it was moving quickly towards me.

I walked towards it, and ten feet further, where the trees were dense from the clouds' darkness, a figure appeared shimmering through the trees. A voice seemed to sing to me, 'Two. Nine. Three. Six ...' all I could see at first was a gigantic surreal smile reaching me from out of the darkness as if out of a Dali melted clock painting, a giant disembodied Cheshire Cat smile. And then came the rest of the face on a wave of eternal light lunging at me.

Tears streamed down my face. "Not now," I told it. "Not now ..."

It was raining incessantly. Will Asha appreciate my fight for her and the entire colony and give me her hand? How could I make her understand that I am just like her, an ordinary boy craving her? Will she be strong enough to run away with me?

Finally, gasping, I reached the love-heart tree.

The rain came in fits and gusts. The sun ran like dappled, pink horses across the land. I ran my fingers through my wet hair. The clouds formed again into dark grey sashes. My heart pounded in my chest. I covered my belongings in a bag to keep them dry and took shelter under the tree. But the rain was moving at so many angles it seemed there was little chance for protection.

My mind jumped through the hoops of hope, desire, doubt, and fear. After many hours of waiting, the skies grew darker and darker. I felt hopeless. I was sure I would get very sick. And it occurred to me, my mind ravaged by that growing storm, that perhaps I was being a careless boy. I thought to myself, I could never get her back.

She never appeared.

I felt my heart, which had once been a supernova star, had now died, to become a black hole devoid of light, tearing its way through some other distant galaxy. I was not there. And yet, I was everywhere, scattered, no longer myself. It was as if every ember of fire within my soul had been doused in water. I felt more pain than death would ever entail. I felt pure nothingness—the absence of existence. The feeling of electricity dying. The sense of a thousand suns being put out. The feeling of nature's beauty and the world being pissed upon, spat upon, burnt to charcoal. Pure and complete loss. I felt the most torturous pain through my entire body, mind, heart, and soul.

My brain shut off. My soul shut off. I felt the kind of intense pain I had never felt before. I would have instead put my hand into a roaring fire! I turned away and walked back like a ghost through the turmeric and galangal bushes in the pouring rain; for the first time in my life, I did not smell their scent, nor felt the rain on my skin, neither felt anything.

For all I knew, Earth had spun wildly out of its orbit. I was numb. The sun could have been stolen from that sky, and I would not have noticed. I was blind. I could see only darkness. Or rather, the absence of light. The world reeled out of its very existence. I saw and felt nothing.

Nothing mattered. All the flowers that bloomed once upon a time within the sunlit recesses of my mind wilted, all the birds of my dreams dropped from their skies to fall upon their backs, and decay to carcasses, and all the sky collapsed upon itself. I was but a dreamer in a dream where there was only the infinite blankness of loss.

I sat and waited for hours and hours; I lost count. But Asha did not show up.

# CHAPTER 28 RELEASE

I arrived back at the river and stopped.

All the years I had spent trapped in the mansion under my father's rule, looking out the window at the outside world, listening to the rain on the glass outside, all those years I wanted to be connected to something. Something more profound, more meaningful than myself. And here I was; this was it. Here I was in the heart and power of mother nature. I was cold; I was wet. The heavy rains continued as I looked at the swaying trees, clouds, and sky, making landslips and battering homes. All the time, I saw flashes of a momentous storm, the moment of water and lightning as the rain pelted my face and my heart. The river swelled with anger. The water had turned into a monster, murmuring and groaning, rolling mud and debris, not knowing how big it was, not knowing where it was going, just moving onwards like a stupid beast destroying everything in its path. Its skull had turned into a delta; its waves were its blood. Like an oaf, it walked through fields, colliding with trees, plowing down homes and huts, and turning everything to ruin. It would not stop till it had wandered everywhere across the land. Suddenly, I no longer felt I had any impulse to move anywhere. I was left with the profound, excruciating longing to shake off this desolate dream.

I felt the weight of depression on my body so severe I wanted only to end the pain, the might of nature unleashing before me, as I watched, as if adrift, as if not there, the rain only lashing my soul. My family, fate, and the universe had taken everything away. And I wouldn't say I liked it; for the first time, I looked upon nature as something to be beaten, something that only took from me and that ought to be destroyed. My heart was full of anger, of bitterness. I felt no resentment. I felt no pain. I felt no love; I felt nothing, just the void.

The rain continued as I shuffled forwards, slipping in the mud. I kept thinking of the image of Asha and the yellow silk ribbon in my head. What was the point of life anymore if she didn't want me? Visions of Paradise kept flooding back to me, making that empty feeling in my gut swell. From where I was now, I could see the dark grey clouds of the storm rolling like a juggernaut over the landscape.

Now the storm transformed the plains into a vast mass of water as the real Paradise floated like a kite in the sky, but some brave youth still swam in it from both sides to look for safer places. Then the smoky grey clouds that filled the sky turned lighter. Occasionally, the sun came out briefly over the waterlogged paddy fields, stretching them into fuzzy light, their silver surfaces shaping imperfect reflections.

In no time, grey clouds in the vicinity dashed against each other, and a series of lightning traveled to the ground lighting the dark sky like the stars lighting the night sky. Peals of thunders followed, thudding the eardrums, and a torrential downpour lashed Paradise. Water gushed through the rivers like a waterfall, causing flash floods.

Water from the gushing Netravati and Gurupura entered houses and residential localities. Large parts of the land were now covered in a newly formed lake.

I turned my head to the sky and asked, 'What should I do?'

# CHAPTER 29 THE FLOOD

I slowed down, almost out of breath, and walked up the dirt path to a lookout over the river. The rising waves washed loose earth from the riverbanks, uprooting rows of coconut trees, and heaving them over the bulged rivers. The stranded men on the banks screamed for their life as the ground gave way beneath them. Above me flew helicopters. Suddenly the entire world and the immediacy of the situation returned to me as if the sound of my life had been until then on mute. Suddenly the sound of the world hit my ears with full force.

Some men away from their huts tried to hold on to their ground, but they were swept into fast, revolving floodwater around tangled coconut trees. Pointing their feet downstream, some of the youth caught hold of long coconut leaves and pulled the remaining men on the top of the spathe, lifting them above the waters. But the leaning coconut trees dangled like swings up and down in the flash floods, terrifying them with bulging eyes. Salvaging their last hope from the top of the coconut trees, they cried out to the heavens for their rescue and spread out wet, red turbans on the coconut leaves. But not sighting the rescue boat in the vicinity, they lamented and covered their eyes as short coconut trees were going under the water. Some limbs splashed amidst the surface, but nothing could be done for lost people.

I got into a larger fishing boat passing by to rescue people from the sinking huts on the river banks. The driver unshackled the bow line from the dock cleat, pulled the rope back to the boat, and drove into the canal a few meters, steering through the swiftly raising waters and the flooded paddy fields in the direction of the stranded people to reach the small mount next to the huts which Paradise overlooked. The engine roared, thrusting the boat forward, raising the bow above the turbulent downstream waters.

Halfway in the middle of the ravaging floods, a powerful whirlpool created by the collision of opposing currents struck the boat uncontrollably, causing tremors all over my entire body. The water currents from the lakes and canals gushing downwards towards the rivers swirled wildly against river currents dashing out from the banks due to the high tides of the seas. The swirling whirlpool created massive bubbles up in huge powerful pushes, large vortices dangerously sucking the boat like a vacuum cleaner, pulling it underwater.

I curled forward my shoulders as the boat swung around the whirlpool once and again. Water splashed the deck, and the vortex grew louder. Soaking in the high waves, I sighted the gaping vortex! The boat momentarily disappeared from my sight. More hallucinations swam through my mind, hallucinations of people, places, and abstract imagery contorting.

I repeated a mantra to myself.

"I will survive this storm."

In a matter of moments, the swirling waters pulled the boat into the outer ring, raising it violently to the top of the whirlpool. As the powerful stream of water threatened to push the boat back into the vortices, the driver steadied it by adjusting the trim to tilt the propellers and accelerated it to climb the walls of water into the flowing stream. The continuous screams for support with waving hands and red turbans from the workers at the riverbanks amidst their plunging in the ever-increasing water levels inspired the driver to gather all his might, and he pressed his hand on the throttle of the boat, swiftly cutting through the upstream current.

Then just as I exhaled a breath of relief, a massive landslide along the edge of the river toppled a row of coconut trees into the river, washing them away and raising a massive cry from the children and women. The young and older men rushed, picking up the children from their huts and pulling them out as the ground beneath them started sinking. The women and men held each other with the children on their shoulders and moved away from the edge of the river holding on to the poles of their huts. But gushing water started washing out all but poles of their blown-away, thatched dwellings.

I repeated the mantra, "I will survive this storm."

# CHAPTER 30 LIBERATE

I threw out fishing nets and ropes from the boat as the driver tied one end of the string to the boat deck.

"Grab hold of the nets!" all yelled. "Grab hold of the nets! Hurry!"

The boat again convulsed forwards and swiftly turned its nose away from the bank. The driver maneuvered the steering away from the spot of the whirlpool, supposing it would suck the boat again. But the currents pushed back the water flowing from lakes, canals, and tailing waters.

Paradise had become Ocean. The sky was turning ever darker. The heavens opened abruptly, water gushed like a tornado, and visibility dropped to a few meters. The boat swayed chaotically, and the driver lost direction in the thick rivulets as the high waves splashed water all over the boat. Then the gushing water from the lakes and canals charged, blasting against the river tides, and the boat almost capsized.

Another wave rolled towards the boat; all I could see was the grey-black beast of the water.

And I was plunged into blackness which retreated into the void, which fled into a dream. And suddenly, I saw

Paradise's blue-grey, stormy skies again. The blue sky disappeared into the grey clouds, and the thunder and lightning zipped past the greenery as if the day was turning into night. The sun hid behind the mammoth clouds that were busy chasing the other without giving any space for the sun to sneak in between. The downpour was so heavy that the overflowing rivers were waiting for an opportunity to engulf the mounts on the island. The riverbanks slowly disappeared, and more water gushed into the fields, and in their fury, many more houses were sucked into it.

Again, I saw a glimpse of the riverbanks and the dark-grey monsoonal sky, and I went under again! I desperately flung my arms around, searching for one of the ropes! But I could not find them! Then out of nowhere, I sighted a dangling, large, wooden plank dipping up and down in the water flow in a swamp far side of the riverbank.

"I will survive this storm."

A massive, freak wave of water hit the boat, sending shards of debris across me; the rain pelted my skin so hard that I was sure it was hail. I reared back for a moment with the dreaded sense of acceleration compacted within a few moments of adrenaline. I could suddenly see myself more clearly than ever before. Colors became more profound and prosperous, and I was sure I could see the immeasurable size of the universe within myself; within that place, I had always felt a nothingness, the place I had always looked for my soul. I could see my life at one point, the love and the fear. Thin strands of light pierced the trees.

I imagined my gazillion atoms launched from my center, destined for the universe's outer reaches. Images of my life flashed through my mind like a roulette wheel, but not just images from my past, images of possible futures, histories, and presents. A beautiful woman in a yellow dress, the chrysanthemum pattern swaying gently in the breeze as they walked along the beach, her smile through the viewfinder of the camera he had once given her, her laugh echoed in his ears, the sway of her hips in the kitchen as she stirred her cup of tea, the scent of orange blossom in her hair. I felt the years all flicker through my mind, and for once, I felt pure bliss. This is what life was about! The feelings! The sensations! The things I was now seeing! The colors! How the sky looked different now from how it ever had before. How the air smelt so much sweeter!

Bubbles surged around me in ascending fits of air. I was drowning! I did not know which way was up. I swam…swam…swam…down…down…down into the depths of this sudden ocean holding on to a wooden plank through the tangles of seaweed and coral till reaching the ocean floor. I found a space in the sandy ground, through which I could see yet again a kind of speck, an ember, as if from a long forgotten underground volcano still glowing. I reached out my hand to grab this ember when I saw, like a plug, that it opened up a new void, a tunnel through which all the water suddenly started flowing! And I was flying through the sky like a bird without wings through clusters of clouds before fading into blackness once more, the void of death.

I could see in a moment in my mind's eye, the banyan tree, a ribbon wrapped around it, and Asha, a swarm of butterflies, first moving around me, then through me, and then I was the butterfly, flying over the hills of some long forgotten land, being pushed by the wind, gliding, all the while flapping furiously over a bed of flowers. The silver sun rose in the east, and suddenly I was in another world again, where dust blew off the group in great wisps, and the sun shone like hot embers. Then the most miraculous thing occurred. At that moment, I was sure my brain had turned off, and I was asleep. But something in me willed me on. Somehow, I realized I was awake in the dream for the first time.

I saw in that instant of time everything moved slower. I felt a high-pitched frequency run up my every bone and dig itself into every pore of my skin. A bright light emanated around me. Like lightning, but lingering. Staying. I could feel my aching, that I was in the last moments before I would let loose; I could see the shivering in my muscles, not just from the cold but from adrenaline, from the fatigue of clinging for my life. I could feel the torrential water rushing over me, my face, and my wet clothes, scattering my hair. And my face was ravished by the winds and the water.

A large wave sent large slabs of debris siding across the land. Again, I did not hear it as the sound of the world seemed mute.

"Grab hold of the nets!" I heard the yell, and shielding the boat behind the trees, I managed to reach out and a hand connected with mine, and with all the strength in my being, I was pulled from the water just as a freak wave hit us from the void of the raging torrent.

# CHAPTER 31 REST

I woke up in the emergency shelter. Some care workers informed me the floods were now slowly easing, but there was much damage. Many people had lost their homes; many lost their lives. It wasn't uncommon for this part of India to be hit by floods. Still, this one seemed particularly bad, and even government buildings and schools were inundated, so it would take time for the area to return to life as usual if it ever could.

While a state of emergency was declared and people rushed to take shelter, there were more days like that, and it was nearly a week before we could get out of the shelter.

I stayed there, huddled in the dark, in a near-derelict building on a remote side of town, in a small community away from Paradise. No one knew me there, and I was glad, for I did not want to be seen or known. I talked to no one but concentrated on rest. I ate the supplies of rice and meager food the rescue workers could offer me. Eventually, as I regained my strength, I helped them sift through and sort out the rubble, debris, and small family items that littered the surrounding area outside the shelter.

I opened the small silver and gold locket with a portrait of my mother inside. It was darkened and worn, almost faded away by the water, and I could not see the image so clearly. The locket was made in America, and I felt her presence, which comforted me. The entire disaster seemed surreal to me.

In those quiet moments, I began to find myself, but I did not want to admit it. I was going through a profound period of self-examination as to who I was. What was my place here in the universe? What was my purpose? And more importantly, what was my purpose here on earth? I felt trapped and helpless; more importantly, I lost myself.

I didn't know why I had to go through such horrible situations, my mother's death, my head trauma, my dad's dislike, Aunt Vidya leaving, Asha's rejection, and the floods. Why did so many events pin me down, one after the other, and why there was only misery in my life after the first eight years? Why am I not able to get what I want and desire? What to make of life after another misery hits life, and there are no clear pathways ahead? Why life felt so cruel sometimes for many people, and how to know and hope that there will be better days? Worst, how to have the strength to find meaning in these cruel events? How to understand these events give us new life and a future? How many people don't have patience and don't want to wait for a bright future after going through such cruel events?

There is no shame in giving up what you believe you have to gain what you do not. Sometimes the most excellent way to gain perspective is not in a new destination but in a new way of viewing your current situation, or sometimes we may need to look at the situation in a completely new way. I did not know what to do or where to go, and my future was no longer certain.

At night, the sky had finally cleared, and I could see the lights of another area of town through the darkened doorway. I left the shelter at dawn. I was still somewhat weak, but I could walk. I put the locket in my pocket and walked toward the town. The road was rather dark, but I continued forward with my backpack. All I knew was that I didn't want to ever return to Paradise.

# CHAPTER 32 DEPARTURE

The world is whizzing by the window of the bus, the markets outside the windows, the asphalt roads covered in light glistening rain. I sat with my backpack in my lap with my damp shoes. My head was resting against the window. The bus was not crowded. Outside I saw an India I had never seen before. And with every minute, I traveled further away, alone from home than I'd ever been.

I felt like a stranger in a strange land.

Outside my window lay a land of still-surging rivers and equally bustling marketplaces. Either on the bus or through the windows, I'd see small children holding cardboard boxes with crayon drawings and schoolwork inside. I'd see women pushing carts piled with stacks of bricks; kids sitting on their backs in a circle as a woman played a fiddle.

This was the first time I traveled on public transport, and the bus stopped at many places picking up and dropping off people, for freshening up, refreshments and meals. There were movements everywhere; people coming in and going, trees and shrubs swaying from the winds, and birds chirping in their world without much botheration, making me known that the world would move on irrespective of situations, circumstances, and worries.

I was carrying a map of the public bus routes and the state's tourist places that were picked up for free at the bus station, but that was it. I read the titles of the many places that the map showed. The titles flowed by like flowers in a river.

For a moment, I didn't feel like a stranger in a strange land; I felt like I was coming home.

As the bus started climbing the Western Ghats Mountains choked by clouds, I saw the sun's rays in the sky but not the sun. At the base of the mountains, I saw a small house among many in the village, its weathered walls falling apart in some parts. A man in a black shirt and white shorts sat outside on a wooden bench. He sat in silence as if trying to drown out the sounds of life from the bus. There was a man with a bullock cart, the ox kicking the air with its hooves as it trudged through the narrow lanes. A woman walked along the empty pathway holding a hibiscus blossom in her hand, its bright red petals swaying with each step. Another woman the next door was drawing up colorful mandalas at the small entrance of her house.

A child peeked out from a carriage held on the back of an ox. A woman standing on her bare feet as she prepared chapattis with her bare hands on an outdoor cooking stove and a three-wheeler carrying countless children from the center of the village to the nearby public school. Yet there was no sign of any worries on any faces. From children to adults, the world seemed to be moving for them in the right direction. I saw the blue sky through the clouds giving them new hope daily.

I thought I would never feel like a stranger in a strange land once I left home. But something inside of me was changed.

I'd seen so much of the land, its rich culture, lush greenery, homes, people, and continuous movement. I felt like a stranger in a strange land.

But still, it's hard to explain how it was possible to feel like a stranger when you are rooted in a place. I did not know where I was going. All I knew was that I was happy to be leaving. And before that moment, I'd never felt so free.

# CHAPTER 33 NEW WORLD

Like slides in a projector, my arrival in Bangalore flashed before my eyes. Gone was the world I once knew, the world of sunbirds, silk, and sequins. All around me, people hustled and jostled.

Standing on the street, I shut my eyes momentarily and let the light illuminate the pink and purple blood vessels in my eyelids; I felt like I was a ghost broken free from the vessel of my body, free to roam over the Earth forever. Only the hum of the city around me reminded me of where I was before someone bumped into me, and I snapped back to reality.

Yes, I was free from my dad's enforcement, but I didn't know how I would survive without the royalty of Paradise. I didn't know how to live away from home or find work, and I knew finding a job wouldn't be easy. But I knew I didn't want to return home, where I had lived so many years in a box. I only wanted to escape for the rest of my leave, not return. Whenever I thought of Paradise, I saw the life I was supposed to have with Asha and my mother, and it was all gone. The only thing I had now to remind me of my mother was her necklace. It was a small gold and silver chain with a golden locket with dimpled edges that made it look like metal ravioli.

I went through the busy streets for a few hours looking around and sometimes stopped in the middle of the street to give way to the magnitude of people crisscrossing every path in the city's center. People were moving everywhere, getting down from so many buses and going about in their world. Many people stood at the corner of a street, raising their heads curiously to see who would take them for their daily wage work as many contractors were busy dealing with their kingpins.

My stomach growls increased, and I couldn't tolerate my hunger anymore. Freedom had its challenges; for the first time in my life, I worried about eating and sleeping. Then I came across a jewelry shop when I turned to the next street; without thinking much, I sold the necklace, though I became emotional when I handed it over to the jeweler. And with that, I relinquished everything associated with my past life.

How long this money would be sufficient, I didn't know, but it gave me breathing space for a few days. That first night in Bangalore, I found a cheap hostel, and I slept on the concrete floor with other travelers, primarily Indian migrant youth workers who were very poor and had very few clothes or even blankets.

For the first time, I met many strangers who couldn't even communicate in the language I knew well. But I could understand their stories as they mostly spoke in the local language I had learned from the low-caste children in Paradise. Each had different stories, backgrounds, and runaway moments due to poverty. Unlike me, they hardly had any education, yet they were hopeful they would find new life in a new city.

Their hope gave me confidence. They didn't have any worries for tomorrow as they were without many things in their life, and they knew things could only get better. Finally, I told them my story in a broken local language, and most laughed at me for running away from the royal life. Some advised me to go back, thinking I wouldn't sustain my newfound freedom for many days. But I was determined to stay put and find out the other side of life even if it meant I had to live like them without most of the necessities.

I was in a new world where everyone escaped looking for freedom from their poverty, and I was no different as I fled to find richness in my life, away from Paradise's royalty.

# CHAPTER 34 FIRST JOB

I was lucky to find a job as a tea server in a central city railway station restaurant to sell tea on intercity trains. Sure, I had always been in between places I felt from the very day I was born. I was always destined for somewhere, and yet I never knew where.

With few other options, I started sleeping at train stations. Sometimes to beat the cold weather, I slept in the empty trains lined up for cleaning at the far end of the station. And when train cleaners saw me, I ran, sometimes ending up in random places where I would sleep in the open air. Between my break, I spent time reading books at a stall that sold second-hand books on the platform, and I sold small souvenirs on the trains, mainly trying to fulfill my hunger for reading or to catch the interest of foreigners. Sometimes I got a purchase here or there, but it was always soul-destroying.

Mostly, the trains took me to places like Mysore, Kochi, and Chennai, but I always seemed to loop back and around and end up in Bangalore, which, if my soul wasn't destroyed already, broke my heart. It seemed I was in an infinite form of purgatory. Again, I wondered how the

Gods were angry with me for being called pure. Was this my karma, I asked, to forever get trapped in this loop of never-ending uncertainty and lack of future hope?

Even still, I saw terrific places like Channapatna, Mandya, Srirnagapatna, Salem, Palakkad, Thrisur, Ambur, Peranmbur, and Puri. I saw lotus and Jagannath temples and flying kites. I saw gurudwaras, mosques, churches, and temples everywhere! This gave me a lot of comfort to my otherwise broken heart and soul, developing my passion for traveling the world and seeing the places. What diversity! I loved traveling by train even if I had little comfort during this time, and I always had to look over my shoulder.

Sometimes when the train stopped in a small village or even a city, I would have enough time to take a flash in my memory from the door of the train or sometimes from the roof.

I had handwritten my CV and given it to a few well-dressed strangers and foreigners I met on the train, but I could never leave my current situation. Time passed slowly. I found myself lost, in a dead-end job, hopelessly sick, and knowing that no matter what I did or where I went, my life was miserable. Somehow, the Gods must not have seen the misery I was going through, or they were angry. Sometimes I was convinced they were laughing at me.

I saw many places and met many people. I marveled at the beauty of nature, different people, and lifestyles, yet sometimes I wondered why I was in such a hopeless situation.

But the romanticism of train travel lulled me into dreams so beautifully through the soundtracks of rhythmic train tracks. Ever since I was a young boy, I have felt more comfortable dreaming than in reality. I was always the one to fall into deep, intense daydreams, whether looking outside through the car window or simply staring into the jungle of paradise. I could not just think in the clouds but live and be in the clouds. Sometimes I thought the clouds were my reality and what others deemed truth was clouds for me.

This job was not without its difficulties, for I had to walk up and down the carriages acrobatically, juggling a jug and a platter of cups, yelling, "chaya chaya chaya!" even late at night. But it presented a problem. Now anyone who has traveled on a train in India knows that there is something absurd about the experience. It is not just the romanticism you see in any train trip in novels and movies. In India, it is a pilgrimage whether you intend it to be or not. It is an experience, and a lesson in knowing yourself, for it, is rarely comfortable being jostled about by chickens and passengers and suitcases, but therein lies the spiritual journey, for it is often when we are out of our comfort zone that we learn the most. But beyond this, anyone who has traveled in India on the trains knows that it is often comical to see passengers who don't have tickets crowd near the already crowded door spaces to make a run for it if a ticket examiner shows up. In my case, I was carrying a platter of hot cups of tea, and when the stampede and the mad rush would happen at the doors, I'd have to contort myself in all manner of twists and acrobatic pirouettes to avoid spilling the tea on myself and others. And all the time, I would call out chaya chaya chaya!

I would still, of course, dream with my eyes open, and when I wasn't serving tea, I was dreaming, and when I wasn't dreaming, I was daydreaming, and when I wasn't daydreaming, I would, after doing the last of the tea, had a chance to talk to the passengers.

I had been interested in spirituality as a young boy in the same way that the monkey or any animal was interested in it. That is to say; I was interested in it without knowing I was curious. I was interested not in any academic sense but only felt something special when I stared up at the sky and abyss of the jungle, watched the clouds, wandered through Paradise, ate the fresh mango from the trees, or listened to the sounds of the birds. There was some sense of a void in every one of those experiences. There was something unending and infinite about every joyful experience I encountered, especially with nature. But now, as an adult and train-tea seller, I was beginning to embark upon the intellectual pursuit of spirituality, a new idea in my mind. I was starting to embark on the mission of learning to understand the jigsaw puzzle pieces of what made those spiritual sensations feel infinite; what was endless, I wondered, and how could I decode that meaning.

In the first few months as a tea server, I was woeful. I nearly lost my job multiple times as the train would rhythmically move up and down, and I would spill the tea. Trying to juggle hot tea on a train at high speed, moving up and down, can make one feel intoxicated. However, as the demand for the job increased, I hardly had time to think about jigsaw puzzles or the division between dreams and reality. There was no thinking of Asha anymore. They just were moments. If I didn't concentrate, I'd spill the tea, simple as that.

# CHAPTER 35 MOVING

In my job, what I liked most was meeting people and talking to them. It didn't matter whether someone was a cook, a beggar, a maid, a priest, or a police officer. I wanted to know them, I wanted to hear their story, I wanted to know what made every individual tick, and I wanted to see the world through their eyes. This helped me not only to understand different views and topics people spoke about and their way of living life but also helped me to sell more tea as I grew in confidence and communication.

I always worked hard, and my boss knew it; sure, I spilled a lot of tea while learning, but slowly, I understood the job's difficulties and learned to love the chaos and the crowds. My boss was happy with me and now posted me on long-distance trains. I visited places I had only ever read about in books or perhaps heard Aunt Vidya talk about. From the chaos of Bombay or the Taj Mahal or the northern lines to the Himalayas, I saw them all, sometimes through the windows of the train, sometimes from the roof, sometimes hanging from the door. It was pretty standard that the trains would break down, depending on the line, but some lines were notorious for breaking down every few days. Often these breakdowns in a new place gave me new challenges, as I would be responsible for ensuring people had tea and were hydrated, and through those conversations, I started selling different kinds of tea. Mind you, I had a jug with three different lids that I could use to pour masala tea, darker tea, or even herbal tea.

And when a train would break down, I would sit with people, and they would often share stories for the sake of it. For the sake of sales, I entertained it, but I think that's when I started to understand the power of storytelling in a community. Usually, people wouldn't talk to each other on a train, especially crowded trains, because who does on public transport? Some people would make light conversation, but that was all. But when the trains broke down, when a situation united people, they came together and talked, and of course, I, the tea server, would be amongst it all, connecting people, guiding conversations. I realized the job was more than serving tea to people; it was about helping people, and it was offering a service.

One day, the train broke down on a railway line from Bangalore to Goa between some jungle, some mountain, some agricultural land, and river beech. This area was known for its beautiful landscapes, like most of India. This place—Gokarna—was very special and famous for its beaches and temples. When the train stopped, we were informed by the conductor that the train wouldn't start again for some time. For many hours people wandered around in the surroundings along the tracks sipping tea many times. Unfortunately, my tea jug became empty very close to that evening, and unless the train started again and reached the following local station, there wouldn't be any more tea. Sometimes that would happen on long journeys, you wouldn't always get a chance to refill the jug, and you could only serve so many people when a breakdown occurs.

So, when we ran out of water, I remember looking out over the agricultural farmland and seeing in the distance what looked like a hut, almost as if I were visiting a mirage of a circus tent. I decided to embark on a journey to see if I could find some water there. And that decision, I didn't know then, would change my life forever. I remember walking across the farm with my jug in one hand and my platter in the other, walking through the dirt. The air was sweet that day; you could almost taste it with the smell of mangoes and jackfruit, and it had something that reminded me of Paradise when I was on my way, walking towards some commune.

From a distance, I could see the river's still waters and the sky dropping far away on the ocean. When I got closer to this large hut, I saw a group of people sitting around it, and they didn't all look Indian. They had lighter skin and looked more like Westerners; they were sitting cross-legged in a circle on the grass. One sat in the middle of the process on a little box, and around him sat a group of what I could only describe as hippies. The man sitting on the box had a guitar in his hand, and he was singing something along the lines of an Indian chant repeating over and over again Shiva Shiva Rama Rama. The image seemed so comical to me; I have to say, as none of the Westerners I met before resembled them. Of course, I met foreigners, primarily travelers, but otherwise, I was still young and left a mostly secluded life, so these Westerners were very surreal. When I walked towards them, the man with the long hair and a tie-dyed shirt playing the guitar stopped strumming, and the other group members turned to face me. This made my right hand rise slowly as if I were meeting a different tribe for the first time and saying hello.

# CHAPTER 36 DIVERGENCE

There was silence all around as a strong breeze from the beach made a rustling sound and blew away the long hair of people sitting in a circle. I curiously looked on for some response, and the guitarist person responded with sprite-like energy, "What are you doing here?"

"Train has broken down and needs water for tea."

"You have come to the right place," said the man with a flat cap. I smiled but replied, "Well, I am looking for water."

Then a young girl with long brown hair from the circle stood up, "It is okay to be here."

Now I felt a little on guard with her politeness, and the wind drew me closer to the circle to assimilate their graciousness.

"Please sit," said another older man, and he made way for me in the circle as if they had been expecting me; it was the most surreal thing. I was pretty bewildered by this, and I knew the train would probably be stopped for an hour more. It might seem strange, but I decided to take a seat. I was pretty mesmerized by the experience, and I was entertained by it, and I thought the universe was holding out its hand to me. I believed I was meant to be there at that moment, and all these people felt it too. I sat down and smiled with my empty water jug, swaying round in the circle.

The guitarist began strumming again from where he paused. After we sang a couple of songs, the man with the guitar said, "Please now fly back on the ground and feel the earth's warmth."

I did that, too, as I thought it would not be nice to walk out of the circle without saying anything to anyone. They seemed so accepting and welcoming. Therefore, the least I could do was stay there with them at that moment.

I felt lost as the music and chanting lasted for an hour, but it helped me realize how good it was to be lost. I felt once again connected to the free-flowing life I had lost since I lost my mother. Perhaps my mother wanted me to connect with hippies for where she had found newness in her life.

I had always avoided feeling lost after my escape from Paradise. Perhaps being lost was precisely what I needed, though. The music and chants they played were incredibly important, as they brought out memories of my childhood connecting to my mother and Aunt Vidya. I suppose when we listen to music with intention, it reminds us of memories; it takes us back to the time, place, environment, and moment in history with its vibes and sounds.

Finally, I remembered when there was a little pause that I was there to get water, so I asked the older adult sitting next to me that is there somewhere I could find some water here, and he said yes. I filled the jug with water, then set off across the field back to the train. Once again, I stopped halfway across the area as the air smelled sweet, still with mango and jackfruit. Then my eyes saw from the distance that the railway track was empty, and for the first time, I needed that to happen. The train had left without me.

I swiftly returned to the group without anyone's notice, as it looked like everyone was obsessed with singing and chanting, and they were in that zone of focus where nothing else mattered. The evening became dusk and the night sky started setting in; the stars brightened their light, awakening me from my memories, but by now, I had forgotten why I was there, and it didn't make sense to catch the returning train at the nearest train station.

At the end of the marathon session, all got up and started hugging me; perhaps they knew how to make me uncomfortable. They were all huge huggers, and this reminded me of my mother, who expressed her love by hugging and caring for everyone and everything around her. My mother's life was all about love, she believed in love setting us free, and indeed love set her free and connected everyone and everything around her. I was too young to understand when my mother was around and when I lost her, I lost everything she lived for and the love that was supposed to set me free. But now I started experiencing the love, though in bits and pieces, as I was getting into that zone after many years, the love that created us and love that brings people closer together even though we are strangers. Now I needed to expand my mind to have the opportunity to see love in a different light, the light that always shines and brings peace and illumination to our life.

I followed everyone to another section of the property to an enormous tent that reminded me of large animal shelters at Paradise. Again, everyone sat in a circle on a mat with a banana leaf in front of them. A pot containing sweet potatoes and a basket of vegetables were passed on from the center of the carpet, and they insisted I eat with them. From my escape from Paradise, I worshipped and ate junk food, which helped me escape my hunger and loneliness. But now I understood how powerful the vegetable diet was, which strengthened my childhood and gave me new vigor to heal my wondered life and look forward to a new direction.

# CHAPTER 37 TALES OF THE WORLD

The man with the long hair and a tie-dyed shirt playing the guitar was a middle-aged man named Leonard. He had a long beard and wispy hair, which made you think that he would've probably been better just going bald. He had a kind of drifting vibe about him as if everywhere he went, he floated like a feather. He was charismatic too. He smiled a lot. I don't think I ever saw him not smiling. Everything made him smile; everything seemed to make him feel some joy that no one else could genuinely fathom and everyone else wanted. Everyone knew that when they saw him, they thought it in themselves, and that's why they were there; that's why everyone was there at the Ashram for this 'spiritual workshop,' as Leonard called it. He told me tales of his world of adventures. He had traveled to numerous countries and been to many different cities.

"How did you end up here in India?" I asked.

"I came for the same reason a lot of other foreigners do. I was interested in enlightenment. My son passed away young, and I was lost. I was completely shattered. I had nothing else, so I found out about a place in India I could go to where I could stay and meditate and reconnect with something other than myself because I knew I couldn't connect with myself. I wanted to escape from myself. I came here to learn about spirituality."

"And did you?"

"I visited many ashrams and met many gurus. I meditated, and I sought solace in nature. And yes, it did help me. Still, there was deep sorrow in my heart. Even though it was not my fault, I felt guilty for my son's death, as he died of cancer, and there was nothing anyone could do."

"So, did you find ultimate healing?"

"Perhaps I'm still on that route, and being here in this Ashram helps me on that path." Leonard then raised an eyebrow, "You smoke?" he asked.

"No," I replied.

"I don't mean tobacco," he clarified as he drank red wine.

I took a sip of my wine. "I didn't think my story was that exciting."

But the more I drank, I felt I had something worth sharing.

"Some time ago," I began, "there was a young girl named Asha, and my soul was looking to fuse with hers as my love flowed for her like water. But my father was against this love as she belonged to a different caste, and I couldn't convince him though he had fallen in love with my mother similarly. I had a roller coaster childhood surrounded by my mother, a foreigner like you. She had come to India to experience newness in her life, and she found that glue in her life, the love that binds everything around us. But I couldn't hang on to that catalyst because I lost her in an accident many years ago."

My first puff of marijuana was not a complete failure. I had never smoked before, and I had never even tried tobacco, so it wouldn't have been any surprise that I choked on the smoke, and the heat of it hit the back of my throat and made me immediately cough. I drew another puff, and enough got into my lungs that suddenly, sitting on the open beach, I saw the stars in the sky abruptly twist as if to say, "Hello!"

I reached out my hand as if to touch the night sky, and for a moment, I was sure I was feeling the edge of the sky and the entire universe. Leonard must have noticed I was looking a bit green because he turned to me and asked, "Hey, Dhaval. You okay?"

"I feel like I'm touching the universe," I replied, not knowing how else to explain it. "Like, there is no distance between me and anything in space and time."

"You say some whacky things, man," Leonard said, mid-drag.

"Dhaval?" said a voice.

I suddenly snapped back to reality, seeing Leonard handing out a joint as if trying to feed me like a baboon.

"What?" I replied.

He pushed the joint back into my hand.

Somewhere in between further drags, I worried I was losing my mind. The thought was quickly replaced by the idea that maybe stars were holes in the sky, and had anyone ever ventured to the edge of the universe to know for sure that they weren't orbs of light? And then, somewhere in amongst those thoughts, I caught up with the idea I had before about touching the edge of the universe and was left with only a sense that it had indeed been a beautiful thought. I realized Leonard had been talking all the while, and I hadn't been listening.

We sat there in silence for a moment before I asked Leonard, "What would you do if you had all the money in the world?

"You know what I've always wanted to do, and one day I will do it. I want to take an old motorbike like an old Norton or Triumph, something old school, and ride from the East Coast of the States to the Californian coast. Can you imagine it? Riding all that way across that continent? Like On the Road," replied Leonard.

"That would be amazing," I replied, and hearing my voice, I was confronted with how polite and formal I couldn't help but sound.

"What would you do?" Asked Leonard.

"I don't know," I replied.

"Oh, come on, you must love something. There's more to you, and there must be something you're passionate about."

"I love writing. And literature. I used to write poetry."

"Poetry?"

"Yeah ... err ... nothing too, you know..."

"You should do what you were born to do," replied Leonard.

My hair stood on end. I felt a humming again.

A constant frequency in my ear.

It was like a static hum. I heard it in the clouded back of my mind. Like an annoying, insistent, continuous sound, it ran like a track through my thoughts, a soundtrack to a movie I couldn't see that never ended. I clung to the storm like it was a solid piece of wood I was sticking to. Leonard lifted me off my feet, laughing like a madman. "We did it. Don't you feel it? The power of being powerful, the power of being human?"

The wind around me ceased, and I realized I had been hallucinating, that I was still on the beach, and the stars were still sparkling in the sky as they had been before I got high. Everything was normal again.

"Wow, that was a strong experience," I said.

"Of course," said Leonard. "But aren't we here to explore our minds?"

# CHAPTER 38 PHILOSOPHY

In the ashram, everyone was a philosopher. They were all there for different reasons. Some came looking for enlightenment, peace, and joy; for others, it was merely an experiment or escapism. Some people wanted to be better at meditation. Others wanted to connect with nature, and some wanted to find something they felt was missing.

Every day, morning and afternoon, in between our sessions of meditation, yoga, music, and chanting, we all worked together in the Ashram and land around in a very touching way. All learned from each other to work in the kitchen, cook, clean, and plant baby trees on the farm, working dutifully even when others learned the work. All had respect and admiration for each other; there was no need to roster any work as everyone stepped in to do every bit of work, living so beautifully within nature as if guided by the invisible hands, moving so gracefully, the hard work in harmony seemed effortless. It was so amazing, and I wondered how it all fell into place.

I came to know everyone by name, Leonard, and all the different people at the Ashram. The young girl Sophie with long brown hair, who had initially made me feel at ease, was from London. She had such a unique look in her green dress. I was mesmerized by her and wanted to learn more about her.

"I want to start a movement!" Sophie said to me when working in the vegetable garden. "Imagine a world without greed! A world without corruption! A world that John Lennon sang about, that Martin Luther King preached about, a world where Jesus Christ lived and practiced servant leadership, and where everyone is equal. There are no borders between states or organizations, or people. A world of complete acceptance. Is it even possible?"

"Why not!" I replied.

"We have everything on Earth needed for everyone's happiness and prosperity, yet we keep making a mess of things. People keep taking more than their share. All these fat cat politicians, you know. Well, I'm sick of it. And let's do something about it."

"So, what's your plan? Get involved in politics?"

"Maybe. Maybe not. It would be a movement to help people understand the simplicity and joy of life in our world. Those who love peace must be just as organized as those who want war," Sophie said. "You know what that means? It means we, the people, don't realize how much power we have. If we come together, we can change the entire world. But that's why they keep atomizing us. They keep separating us from ourselves. To disperse us because they know if we join together and get organized, the whole structure of the world as we know it will flip on its head!"

One evening, Sophie and I looked out at the stars as the golden glow of the distant city leaked into the sky. The atmosphere was serene and calm. We climbed up the mound, and all around us were the pot plants we all worked on during the daytime. There were cherry tomatoes, sage, parsley, and chili peppers, but the plants were getting colder as it was late autumn. Some leaves of the turmeric plants were getting bronze-tipped. We sat there in silence, feeling as though we were hovering above the world, in some ancient Babylonian gardens where ivy crept around the walls and all around us. It was dark by then, the street lamps had turned on, and it was almost like we were in a private world. No one knew we were there. We were enjoying the serenity and silence.

"I guess I came chasing the spiritual experience, you know," said Sophie.

The day's heat had faded only slightly, and warm tendrils of river and ocean air seemed to ravel and unravel within my nose. Someone had already started the bonfire on the riverbank, and a few of the Ashram mates had circled it. The moon lit up the silhouettes of the trees that dotted the bubbled dunes. We slowly walked down to the bank and cut across the sand in its fluorescence. A little further, where the path collapsed into the dunes, we sat down on a small clean patch of sand hemmed by a blanket of marram grass and looked out over the river and the distant ocean. It was still drizzling. The wind ripped at the face of the river turning the crests of the waves as white as the full moon. The lights of a few ships scattered on the ocean blinked on the horizon, shining like marbles in the moonlight.

The white crests of the waves blurred. Sparrows swarmed above the distant fields. The grass bordering the dunes danced like sea anemones in the wind, stretching their spindly fingers to the sky. The sand flowers closed up their petals for the night. The seaweed floating on the surface of the shore tangled upon itself and swam like electric eels chasing their own misshapen static. Amongst the grass that bordered the beach, we lay down on a soft pillow of sand, peacefully watching the purplish black night-time sky. Few people were around that bonfire as others were on their way back to the hut.

The small and bright ship lights felt like fallen stars that had come down to Earth and refused to die, so they were now floating on the horizon. The whole world around me felt like a hug, and I felt at peace, a peace I had not thought about for a very long time. But this was a different peace anyway now; it was a peace that did not come from without but within, a peace I had conjured up within myself. Lying on the sand, I tilted my head back. The sky was clear, and the stars shone so magnificently.

# CHAPTER 39 PASSION

Sophie buried her head in my lap, and I stroked her hair and tossed her wild locks. Sophie told me her hair was like this due to her "no-poo movement."

"No-poo movement?"

"Let me tell you the story behind it" Sophie raised her head and clutched my hand. "My parents thought I was studying politics," said Sophie. "Truth is, I gave it all up when I moved to London and took up work, ten-hour shifts six days a week, in a supermarket."

"What do you do now?" I asked.

Sophie explained how she had first moved to London from Scotland to study acting before realizing that acting wasn't for her, and it made much more sense in a world where money means everything, to pursue finance instead. Good, her parents said, their daughter could go less wrong with finance than arts. However, Sophie only got halfway through her economics degree before explaining to her parents that it wasn't for her. She had decided that the world of financial advising, investment, or banking wasn't for her either. Instead, she had decided that she wasn't academic and was born to be a cop. Halfway through her course, despite top marks, she had decided that she didn't have what it took to be a cop and instead chose to become a baker. Fine, her parents said, this time, complete what you set out to do. She completed two whole years of her baker apprenticeship, and just when she had progressed to making croissants and pecan pastries, Sophie announced that she had made a mistake again and that baking wasn't for her, but neuroscience was. She said it was a great idea because she realized that she had always been interested in the brain and how it responds to certain situations (like stress for a police officer or getting up early to bake bread.) In many ways, she said, everything she had done so far was, in a way, good training for the field of neuroscience and philosophy. And it was all a life experience.

Her parents responded that they had spent enough money and time supporting her. If she wanted to travel to Athens, they would not pay for or help her, and she would have to support herself. Having had enough of her foolishness, they threatened to turn their back on her altogether. They suggested that working in a bank could help her build her finances. Perhaps, she could go to church on Sundays? Maybe she could be more like her older sister, marry, and have three children. Sophie accepted the reply calmly and explained to them that she had already booked a ticket to Athens, that she had finally found her true passion, told them she had dumped her long-term boyfriend, gave them the roundabout address of a friend she said would be staying with on her couch to start with, and not to worry about her, and indeed, not to call her till she called them. Her family could hardly stop her from doing what fate had already done.

And she never called.

"So, I studied philosophy in Athens, the land of great philosophers. And though I wanted to be a philosopher, I started working at an NGO. Now I'm here in an Ashram, chasing kundalini awakening. What about you? What's your story?"

"It's a long story," I replied.

"But what do you want to do?" Asked Sophie.

"I want to travel the world," I replied.

"And what will you do in the meantime?" asked Sophie.

"I will do what I think I want and explore the world as I need," I replied. "I don't want to travel the world, and I don't want to tick off countries. I want to experience life."

"And what does it mean to you to experience life?" asked Sophie.

I thought for a few seconds and found myself admitting I knew what it meant to experience life for the first time. In many ways, I had spent a lot of time wondering about that very thing. But now I was convinced I knew. "To me, it meant living without holding anything back. It meant dancing like no one was watching, reading poetry out loud for its sake, reading great books, drinking great wine, and sometimes bad wine and laughing about it, and sometimes running through fields of grass with bare feet."

"And stepping on a mine? Or worse, a tick!"

"Ah, now you're just being cynical!" I spoke. "Seriously, I want to do what you are already doing. You went for it; you decided to leave everything behind; you left your world and explored another. I guess I want to be spontaneous and free and experience life and know the truth without getting in the way of thc truth."

"And what truth is that?"

"I don't know yet," I said.

"But I guess you're at a point in your life when discovering your truth," said Sophie.

"What if there's no truth?" I asked.

She got up, looked at me for a moment, and laughed, "The journey of a thousand miles begins with a single step. And if you take that single step, and decide to change, then

I guess, and this is just my personal opinion, that's when you start to get your feet on the ground."

"So, I'm supposed to live without overthinking about it."

"Yes," she said.

"And what if I'm wrong?"

"Then you would change your mind," she said, smiling.

"Do you believe in free will?" I asked.

"I believe in the freedom to choose," she said, and then she looked at me again and said, "I believe in making mistakes and learning from them. I believe in creativity and intuition, and the courage to be. And I believe in waking up every morning and having a new chance to get it right."

I smiled. "We make our meaning, right?"

"Exactly," she replied.

That night we stayed up all night talking till everyone had left, and the fire was mere embers, and all that remained with us was the glimmer of the moonlight on the water's edge until we gently fell asleep on the sand, hand in hand.

"How would you describe this place in one word?" Sophie asked.

"In one word?" I replied; I needed to think about it for a moment, deeply, while I looked out at the blinking lights on the horizon. "Ataraxia."

We kissed.

# CHAPTER 40 FREEDOM

Sophie said there were three freedoms we needed in life; freedom from corporations, freedom from religious extremism, and freedom from moreism. Moreism is the thing that is ruining the world. People want more, more, and more. We are living in the age of exponentialism. That is the cult of exponential growth, and she was sick of it, and she said she couldn't completely understand why no one else was as sick of it as she.

She had big ideas about the world that seemed sophisticated, edgy, and always full of insight. She had a certain magnetism I couldn't get enough of. She was always passionate about things and had views and opinions that one could change. But you had to earn that change of mind, which was difficult. I started to realize I liked people like that, people who had opinions and thought deeply about things and who were conversationalists and loved a good debate but never an argument. I realized that was the person I am too.

She showed me films on her mobile and music. We sometimes talked for hours when meeting impromptu in the garden. Sometimes we cooked together. She was a great cook and believed in exploring everything life offered. She gave me music from all around the world. After all, she was a DJ. Mostly, it was African music. Fela Kuta, Saleif Kita, those kinds of giants in African music. But there was other music, more obscure stuff she found in the back of a crate in an old forgotten vinyl scope. Somewhere in Camden or some different hip quadrant, modern and old stuff, everything from Zaid Rahbani to Sebastian Tellier to Cesaria Evora to Tony Allen. That was the kind of person Sophie was. There was not a single taste she didn't like, and that meant she found gems in all music genres. She tasted all food. She often would sit back on the top of the mound, mid-drag or sip of gin and tonic, and say, "You know what I love, watching everyone caught in their pedantic everything."

Sophie liked to have discussions and debates. I still don't understand why this concerned her, but it was. She said she enjoyed these conversations and that they were essential for understanding what was happening worldwide. Sometimes we would get lost, out of ideas, arguing and fighting, talking and thinking for hours. In our opinion, the greatest threat to humanity was not all those villains on the world stage but rather the people who believed. The people who come together for a big fight but never really reach a resolution, the constant stream of pointless arguments that happen within the minds of people who claim to love one another. The belief in a moreist superiority over other moreists and the lack of passion, enthusiasm, and mutual love that makes us human beings who enjoy only the best things in life. Moreism.

What followed was a process of reinvention. I decided to change everything about myself. And I mean everything. Was I unhappy with my previous self? Yes, and more. I was disappointed with my entire life. Somewhere and sometime, I felt like my life had been like a train and had derailed off the tracks it was meant to follow. It was constantly spinning out of control, and there seemed to be no plan to get me back on track. I had a unique outlook on life. I believe it's a matter of attitude whether we're in a good place or not. But back then, I was stuck in my mind, and I felt I needed to shed my skin like a snake. It had dawned on me that I was free from my father, caste, and name. I could be whoever I wanted to be. Something new opened up for the first time in my life, and I was alive with imagination and wonder. At night I would lie on my mat and think of who I wanted to be, and I would try to will it into the air. In some ways, this might sound like I was selfish. I supposed I was. I was self-obsessed because I felt I had to be; I had to put in the mental work to truly free myself from every limitation I had ever accidentally taken upon myself. I vowed to discover the truth and not just what I felt I had to do because someone told me it was right. I vowed to find myself and discover my true self and passions. I was going to make something of myself, I told myself. I was not content to be a nobody. I was going to become truly remarkable, and it wasn't even a question of fame or money. I wasn't interested in those things. I was interested in feeling the depths of my existence. I was always a voracious reader and have read a book a week since the age of ten for many years. Now I was reading self-help book after self-help book. I started consciously focusing on the art of learning. I realized that if I could teach myself to learn, I could become limitless.

I knew that in breaking away from my father, I was breaking away from university and the academic path of life. I knew that the path that my father had planned for me was the path of business, and I wanted to change all of that. I didn't want to be a businessman. I knew I had a passion for being a writer or perhaps a philosopher from now onwards. I also knew that I was entering an age in which university was about to change forever. I knew that all the information was waiting for me, and I could access it with sufficient willpower. And as far as I was concerned, I did not lack that. I was determined like never before.

I justified what I was doing by saying that I would return to my father one day, but it would be when I had made something of myself on my own back. I needed to create something with my life.

I started dressing in new clothes, reading more and more, and learning how to find new people, impress them, and enter their world. While university might have given me a framework for learning, in many ways, I can safely say I could still get to the university. However, I didn't need that framework. I had unknowingly built my framework from a young age, and as an adult, I was still actively working on making that system. It was a true passion. I saw a chance to learn from everyone and everything. Life was my university. Everyone I met was my teacher; everything in front of me was my teacher. It was so much more than learning a subject, learning about a topic, and learning from it. This was an all-inclusive education. My attitude to learning was also one of a mature person, one who was worldly and already had many pieces, the background, the insight, and the understanding.

# CHAPTER 41 OTHER HALVES

There was freedom in Sophie's movement and speech. She was liberated. She did what she wanted to do, and she never held back. And I think, looking back on it, that's the thing I fell in love with most. After that, mainly during that period, my only thought about her was that this girl was different from Asha. It was divergent energy, anyway. A different kind of electricity because she explored the world, explored life, explored nature by getting and creating opportunity.

This time when I saw her, she was wearing a yellow summer dress, utterly different from the sleek black numbers I had only ever seen her wearing as if she were a ninja, and she took my breath away.

Sophie and I walked to the shore in silence. It wasn't the kind of silence that is awkward or anything, but comfortable silence lovers fall into when nothing needs to be said.

We knew we were attracted to each other, and this time she unveiled her love philosophy.

"Greek mythology confers that humans originally had two faces, four legs, and four arms. Zeus, the king of Greek Gods, split the humans into two parts to mitigate their excessive power, challenging them to devote their lives to find the separated halves."

"What is this Greek mythology anyway?"

"You know what Plato said about soulmates?" said Sophie. "Humans were created androgynous at the beginning, partly male and female. Both sets of sexual organs existed in early humans, with four legs, two faces, and hands. These humans were monsters moving very fast using their legs and hands like a cartwheel. Thus, they were mighty, making the king of God nervous, fearing the domination of humans. To punish the humans for their rebellion, Zeus, king of the Greek Gods, cut them into two parts and, through his son Apollo, turned their faces towards their cut part to remind them of their wound for better behavior. Then Zeus pledged to cut them again if they continued their threatening behavior. Next time, humans would be hoping around with only one leg, bringing absolute misery to humans. This made each cut half of the human to long for the other half, hugging each other, intertwining to become whole again by growing together."

"Then Zeus showed pity on humans to have some satisfaction when embracing by turning their sexual organs to the front. The cut and detached humans made children by casting seeds in the ground like cicadas and not in one another, and this prompted Zeus to turn the sexual organs to the front." She continued, "Therein the foundation was laid for us to desire and love each other. Love is, therefore, innate for every human being and unites us with our original other half, making two parts into one by healing the wound of the division of human nature, hence the desire to seek the other half. This innate love discovers one's soulmate by finding the other half to complete the whole person. Greek philosophers agreed that humans are fundamentally wounded. Thus, humans are likely to exhibit fatal conducts that seem entrenched. Therefore, we are doomed to keep searching for our other halves."

"But what if Plato was right and wrong simultaneously?" I questioned.

"Perhaps it's not our bodies that were split in two; it was our souls," Sophie responded, gazing into my eyes. "We shouldn't feel embarrassed. Deep down, we're all clowns; we're all beautiful idiots, fools, and jesters trying to make our way in this crazy world. What holds us from being ourselves and letting go? We're so afraid of the trauma of our childhoods that we revisit it over and over, trying to resolve all the shit that, back then, we didn't understand. Our view of the world was me, me, me. That's all there was. So, someone criticizing something you did wrong was a reflection on you. The tragedy is that it takes an entire lifetime to escape from that for some people, and some never escape it. I mean, isn't it crazy that we fear every day stepping outside, that we'll get eaten by a shark if we surf that wave, or we'll get hit by a bus if we walk across the road with our eyes open?"

"That one probably makes sense."

"But all the while, we are being eaten up from the inside, run over by a thousand buses that are our childhood traumas, unconsciously tangling us up over and over as we try to resolve issues from our past that were never really issues in the first place. We are all personal human beings, and we just put these layers and masks upon ourselves, you know? That's what's helped me so far to heal this stuff, realizing that I don't need to become intimate; I need to shed the bullshit that stops me from being intimate, which is what I truly am. And being completely and utterly honest with people from the start, no matter what the consequences are."

# CHAPTER 42
# RELATIONSHIPS

You know, the ancient Greeks had six words for love. It's like the Inuit have ninety-nine words for snow because they needed those specifics; snow matters more to an Inuit than an Australian. What if the ancient Greeks understood love in a way we've forgotten? What if that alone was why the Greeks could philosophize and think up things that were arguably ahead of their time? Being intimate isn't just about sex or romance. It's about being close to others, emotionally whole, building emotional intelligence, and being intimate with the world.

So many people are addicted to romantic love when that is just one fixation of an idea of love.

Love is everywhere. Love for family, love for friends, love for nature, love for certain things, and so on. Sometimes when we try to find love only in certain things or romantically, we might get confused or get our hearts broken because we search for particular love rather than experiencing love in everything we do and relate to. However, broken and disjointed love blossoms once again when we experience love everywhere and in everything.

Maybe that's what we're doing here. We may not find perfect love at once or perfect love in anything. Love is a process rather than a program. In that process, sometimes we get broken, get confused, and our hearts get broken to find honest and true love, yet love continues to bloom when we have a desire for love, like a flower flourishing from the bud, because that's what love is.

It was dark in the surroundings by that time, and the moon was sneaking out on the horizon. My mind churned. My breath was short and dry, and I felt a lump in my throat and a glass bubble in my mouth.

Sophie and I kissed again, and I spun her around in my arms. She unbuckled my pants as we continued spinning, dancing in the cosmic orbit of each other, in the orbit of more lust and less love. We undressed in a flurry, flinging our shirts onto a shrub, a pair of underpants on the footwear, and made love on the grass patch of the dry riverbed. And suddenly, there she was again. And there I was. Naked in all our beauty, in the soft moonlight. We were exposing our souls to each other, without armor, trying for fusion.

Though this was the first time I was having sex with a woman, I never felt anything similar when Asha and I were rolling below the coconut tree; I never felt like the heavens were opened for us! Sophie was as beautiful as Asha, and our naked bodies intertwined like those snaking rivers, yet it seemed more about lust than love for an attractive Sophie. In desire of the body, I felt the touch of skin upon the skin and her lips upon mine and her, full of such primal energy! It seemed she wanted to grab life by the horns and make it hers to own. And I was drawn to that and felt feminine power in her rather than binding love. I could feel that our hearts were never connected when we made love as the entire world seemed to stop in its rotation and time seemed to stop, the night singing birds put on hold, the moon suspended in its orbit to witness only the two bodies coming together but not two souls.

That night we slept under the stars that shone above all of Ashram. The air was warm and the air smelt of mango and Indian beer. Yet I knew I couldn't connect my soul to Sophie's; perhaps the body's desires had overtaken the soul's passions to connect with her body, but I could feel that there was no real love.

"What if that God is the Fates?" Sophie questioned.

"In that case, it wouldn't matter if you found your other half."

Sophie laughed. "So, what do you think you were looking for?"

"I wasn't looking for the better half," I said.

Sophie laughed again. "How do you know that?"

"Because our souls didn't connect, it was a pleasure to the body, a real pleasure I felt for the first time, but I could feel there was no pleasure to the soul at all."

"You're already a philosopher?" Sophie teased me.

"No, it's just ... I don't want to believe in fate. I want to believe in something more than fate, you know. A grand synchronicity to all things that explains everything; what we're doing here, where we're going. The desires of the flesh alone would never bring us to our better half, and when you end up going after the flesh, it will hurt your soul. Perhaps, just perhaps, a broken or wounded soul will never be united with the body to find a better half and ultimate love?"

"Perhaps that was the reality for me, I went after the desires of the flesh without connecting with the desires of the soul, and I am yet to find my better half after many relationships."

"Sometimes what we do may be good for our body but may hurt our soul, and all that we do would have consequences."

"You think there are consequences in life?"

"Of course I do. How could I not?"

"What do you mean?"

“I mean, haven't you ever thought, what if our lives weren't meant to be like this? What if we were not meant to be together, but something went wrong, and in one moment, I made a mistake, and you ended up with the wrong man, not because of love but because of desires of the flesh?”

"Then can love to be temporary and still beautiful not because of its permanence?”

“True love is permanent and everlasting, and the union of both body and soul can only experience such love”

# CHAPTER 43 TRANSIENCE

I remember the night when everything came to a head. Sophie and I had reached the end of the line. Lying on my bed, I remember staring at the ceiling and wondering what everyday life would feel like because I knew I had never lived a normal life since my eighth birthday. And what is normal anyway? I don't think anyone ever knows; all I knew was that whatever it was, I was far from it. Somewhere along my life path, something had taken away a part of myself that had broken away from me.

I looked up and saw the moon through the overgrown jasmine bushes. And like the ghostly figure I once saw looking over my shoulder, the moon watched me. I remember it was raining and a faint mist through the trees.

I could see her standing in that mist for the last time. The moonlight made her brown hair glow like copper, and I tried to find the strength to tell her, "Don't leave."

And I know memories are only memories of memories, but I remember everything about life in Ashram and with Sophie though we were not soulmates. Indeed, we were best friends. I remember how we talked for a very long time. At times we cried. She asked me questions. I answered. I asked her questions. She answered. I realized how attached to her I was to find answers to my questions. Since my mother's death, she was the only one to whom I could find some of the answers, and she brought out from me some of my solutions for both of us. She was mysterious, pretty, and intriguing.

Most importantly, she matched me on an intellectual and philosophical level. She gave me so much knowledge. And I gave her insights. Together we were lovers of wisdom.

At times, I was sure I felt the ripples of her thoughts in my brain as if we were tuning into each other's frequencies. It was only then that I realized I didn't know what I was thinking and that if I were a radio, I would be just white noise in Sophie's ears. So I readied myself; I tried to focus on the moment, what was going on, and what it all meant. I willed time to slow down enough to understand my life's storyline. How hard it was to put my thoughts into words when I was thinking so much about it, placing pressure on the idea of it, how difficult it was to communicate and to understand. And yet, for all my efforts, my mind seemed to slow, time seemed to slow, and my mind seemed lost in a fog. Suddenly I saw the world had become dim too as if I were walking through a blizzard of white, the same nothingness white I had seen in the hospital so many years ago when I had thought I had woken up in an atomic bomb.

Sophie told me she would return home while she could, as her parents are now searching for her internationally through social media platforms and various embassies. "They have come to know that I am in India through the Scotland immigration officials, and it will be hard for me to hide anymore."

I offered to go with her, but she said she needed to return alone. I remember the last time I saw her at the train station. Perhaps if I had gone with her, my life would have run an entirely different course, but I didn't. And maybe that was my fate.

"I have to go home, Dhaval," said Sophie.

"I know," I replied.

"And I don't want to keep you waiting."

"I know," I replied.

That night, I felt utterly alone for the third time.

# CHAPTER 44 RETURN

I felt lost and set to drift forever without an anchor in a stormy sea. I plunged further and further into the sea of depression. Time sped up, and time slowed down. I repeatedly woke up as if from a long sleep and wondered where I was. All that new life that Ashram had given me looked temporary. I couldn't do the regular duties of the Ashram like before. Separation after separation that layered around me didn't allow me to socialize with Ashram mates anymore, and I didn't know what to do. No talks, inspiration, and counseling by elders at the Ashram helped me to accept my current situation, and one day I slipped out from the Ashram without anyone's approval, not that I needed one. Still, lowness in life didn't allow me to bid goodbye more respectfully.

Once, it was at a bus stop, once in the park, and once in a shop. Every time, I woke up in a new random place. I looked at my hands and reminded myself of the journey of my life that reinstalled the memories of my life back into my head. Sometimes I experienced countless nightmares; other times, I dreamt I was a butterfly, the brilliant blue of mosque roofs flying through the sky.

Slowly time seemed to pass into a dream. I lost track of the days, and everything became a blur. I spent many days like this, but even then, in the lowest pits of my despair, I realized I had to take control of my life.

After some time, I fell into a dream and got on a local train without knowing where I was headed. The scenery lulled me, and strobing light flittered out by the window, the sun hung low in the sky over countless paddy fields, and I could see it strobing through the coconut and palm trees lined road toward Goa.

At each station, the rush of the crowd filled the train to the brink, making me wonder what Goa had so special in store. I arrived at the train's final destination, the Karmali railway station. It was full of people trying to move in one direction, which amplified my curiosity, and I joined them walking along, brushing shoulders with many.

I noticed people walking in reverence, repeatedly muttering some sentences similar to the mantras we recited at the Ashram. After some distance, I could see a tall structure with delightful art and rich Architecture, and it didn't take long to understand it was a church similar to the one I attended my mom's funeral service.

Suddenly the people started queuing up from a distance, and as the queue moved at a languid pace, I was looking to interact with people around me. A visitor from the US gave me an insight into why so many people were there. "I am here to see the remains of 16th-century saint St Francis Xavier's in-corrupted body. The saint was an incarnation of love, peace, and truth, and I can feel that energy here today."

"What? More than four hundred years ago, someone had died, and his body is still in-corrupted?"

"Many saints' in-corrupted bodies throughout the world witness their sacrificed life to better the world with love and charity."

Seeing the people's amazement, I thought deeply to make sense of what he said. By now, I had developed some of that amazement and curiosity, and the slow-pace walking for more than a kilometer went unnoticed. As we approached the relic, some people knelt; others touched the glass box and kissed through their hands; most were busy taking photos through their phones. I went on observing everything and the minutest of details, but strangely I didn't experience anything like the American visitor.

"Why do people fake their experiences? If they are not faking, why didn't I experience at least a minuscule of it?" I questioned as I left the place as quickly as possible and returned to the train station, for I couldn't take any more lies.

I wanted to find the answer to the fake stories of people and the world. I remembered another such event of the big crowd during my tea-serving job on the Garib Rath train from Bangalore to Puri Jagannath Temple. However, I didn't have any inspiration to visit the temple at that time. This time I was a traveler like any other, and a thirty-five-hour journey on the train, at that age, felt like an eternity. I went through all the stages of any long journey; boredom, interest, sleep, half-dozing, more sleep, and more lethargy.

Finally, I gave up worrying about the time and drifted into a deep slumber. When I woke up, I saw the scenery had changed as we arrived in Puri. But my goal of finding answers superseded everything, and I went straight to the temple. Before long, the Jagannath temple appeared majestically through the trees, towering over the ancient city sprawling at its feet where cyclists and rickshaws dodged the pedestrians and vendors pursued pilgrims. Fearless monkeys scampered wherever they pleased. Roars of adoration from a sea of devotees emanated intermittently from the temple's innermost shrine. Wafts of incense camphor and ghee lamps filled the temple.

"Jai Jagannatha!" the crowds chanted. I soon entered the cobbled temple compound and stood behind the famed Garuda pillar; I caught a glimpse of Lord Jagannath. Countless devotees tried to inch closer to the deities along the guardrail, beyond which only priests are allowed. The massive gods were in their tribal forms, with huge eyes, attired in gold and decorated with jewels and flowers. A priest appeared and gestured for me to step forwards to the pillar. I was frightened. His eyes haunted me the most, for they were the only part of his body that did not somehow give way to his eccentricity. His eyes seemed to lock on to whatever he looked at, unbudging, always focused. "It's time to embrace the pillar," the priest said, nodding at me to say it was okay to touch it.

"I'm scared," I told the priest.

"It is just a pillar, and thousands touch it every day. There is no reason to worry; Lord Jagannatha will bless you."

I looked again at him, concerned. The priest again beamed a smile and gestured to the pillar. "Touch it," he repeated, knowing this was the moment everyone had traveled so far for. I put out my hand tentatively and, closing my eyes for fear of what was about to happen, placed my hand upon the pillar. With my hand still touching it, I looked back at the priest. But I felt nothing, nothing at all.

Again, I rushed from the temple to the train station and found a way to the nearest Jama Masjid, which attracted me with its majestic architecture, yet again I felt nothing from within.

I was hoping for something mind-blowing, a paradigm shift, a holy bolt of lightning from at least one of the religious places of temples, churches, or mosques, but what

I got was nothing. I couldn't even experience and understand any of these so-called experiences and wondered why. I looked at statues, altars, paintings, and deities and could not find one difference; they all looked the same. I don't know what I was hoping for when I went up to the big, orange god and said, "I wish to attain enlightenment!"

It would look at me with those bluish-green eyes, and bam! That's it. I had nothing.

As you can imagine, I wanted answers, but there was nothing at the temple, nothing at the church, and nothing at the mosque. There was no answer. So, nothing happened? Nothing.

# CHAPTER 45 NEW FOCUS

I became madly focused on learning everything that was a lie in the world, everything that was a misconception or a myth. For it seemed so much of my world was a lie. Everything I had been taught and everything people said was expected in the world, I now realized, was primarily the result of particular insanity.

Everything was backward, from how I was told to breathe to how I was taught to eat to how I was introduced to walking. And I said to myself I was done with it. I wanted to be free from it all. I wanted to experience life and truth for myself and not from others, to be free from all illusion, and to live a life of pure clarity.

There were no more dreams, illusions, or wandering around. I wanted to focus on the truth of the world, an absolute truth, not relative anymore, and put my life and soul into finding it. I wanted to explore everything, the great writings, the scriptures, the philosophy, the science, the religions, the political systems, the social systems, the economy, and all that by reading, listening, watching, and meditating. And that was my only focus, and nothing else mattered.

I returned to Bangalore and visited Moorthy's second-hand book-selling stall, where I used to visit and skim through the books between my tea-selling job on trains. This time I wanted to grasp all the writings and analyze and discern myself to find the truth and not skim through any book. But to my pleasant surprise, Moorthy offered to help me put up a new stall very close to the new university campus that had just been built on the outskirts of the city, and this helped me not only to read all the books but also earn my living.

Moorthy divided the books into two wooden carts and offered one cart and half of the books, hired a mini truck, and put up the book cart near the university campus entrance. He offered to provide new second-hand arrivals from his contacts every week. I rented a bed space near the university where mostly cleaners and helpers of the university lived. This helped me to be near the cart most of the time and understand some of the know-how of the campus from those workers.

The market for second-hand books is quite significant in India, where people sell or exchange read books many times in different parts of India and sometimes century-old books. Like a tourist, these books travel the length and breadth of the country, exchanging many hands as long as they are reasonably maintained. Even the printing errors on the cover page or the sample books landed them in the second-hand market, and people had choices to buy some of the sound, new-looking books for low prices. When they finished reading, they exchanged them for another new read for a few hundred rupees. This circle of exchange provided massive stock of books for second-hand booksellers on the cart, giving them quick bucks, and benefitted the readers with their hobby without spending much money.

This job came naturally to me since I was an avid reader; every day, I read at least one book from start to finish and skimmed through a couple of other books. When students, lecturers, and visitors passed through the stall, I vocally told them why they should read a particular book, which pages have those interesting passages creating amazement in them. Hundreds of books were sold daily, and many returned every other day asking me which book they should buy next. In that process, dialogues became a daily routine, where many joined to listen and sometimes exchanged views that went on for hours in the evenings as most of the students and lecturers lived on the campus. Many of the readers returned the books once they finished their reading and exchanged them with the new arrival of second-hand books every week, and my profit became multifold in no time, which helped me to pay back Moorthy in a short time.

As the business flourished in no time, the space wasn't enough for thousands thronged to the cart, and university management was happy to lease a shop on their premises next to the coffee shop, and this soared not only mine but the coffee shop revenues by multifold. I now leased out a one-room accommodation which gave me more liberty to do my stuff, especially reading more.

But more than the culture of reading, gaining knowledge became the new norm, with every weekend, students coming together to debate and exchange views on particular books and their influence on life and society. The area around the bookshop became a mini theatre on weekends with debates, mini-acts, and dialogues. Many became my close friends, exchanging ideas, and I felt like one among them, though I wasn't a student. As the students' inflow increased every weekend, the informal dialogue became formal, with few students taking leadership to organize the debates. They assigned different topics weekly, such as philosophy, religion, politics, science, and economics, and arranged different speakers and awarded the best debates and acting.

I mostly debated in philosophy and raised questions to the audience, creating deep thinking in them. Why do people desire diamonds? Because a company a hundred years ago convinced people of their worth? Why do people gargle mouthwash? Because a company a hundred years ago convinced people this was a good idea. Why do people shave their armpits and legs? Because a company a hundred years ago convinced people this was a noble idea. Students filmed some of these debates, which went viral on campus, and many students exchanged their views and publicly expressed their stands on social media.

The finding of the debates for many, including me, was that we need to ask questions to get to the bottom of the truth. I learned from some lecturers and students that they happily debated such questions related to their subjects in similar ways, but few were against this "new sense," as they called it. There were murmurs that some cult thinking had invaded the classrooms, which had diverted the set syllabus and topic of the lectures. The lecturers and students against these debates were furious that the university was moving in a new direction without any direction from the top management. This set out the protests for and against, and high-decibel voices started echoing in many classrooms and breakout areas.

As I had experienced in life, I learned that change was quite challenging for many. And yet again, my new-found life hung in the balance.

# CHAPTER 46 HURDLE

Suddenly everything in my life turned on its head once again. The viral videos of the debate and questionnaires reached the top management and then the University leadership, and there were whispers that I would be called in for questioning. Though I had developed much confidence now, I was nervous not knowing which direction the management would tilt. All sorts of thoughts came into my mind, mostly negative because of the protests against the dialogue. What if they stopped these debates, canceled the bookshop's lease, or asked me to leave the premises and surroundings altogether?

Soon the whispers came out to be accurate, and I was summoned to meet the management the next day. I didn't know how to prepare, though student leaders, who supported me in the continuation of the newfound dialogue and questionnaires at the university, sat with me, telling me how to face the management and answer their queries. I listened to all of their suggestions, defending their and my take on why we should continue this new-found initiative at the campus. Yet I wasn't confident enough to face the management, perhaps for lack of formal training in any field or education, nor had I attended any interviews where my intellect, communication, or knowledge was tested. I spent a sleepless night in anxiety, meditation, and mantras using the methods my Aunt Vidya once taught me to focus on the task.

The next day there was much chaos when I walked towards the management office; students who were in the recess shouted slogans both for and against me, though the voice of support was louder than the dissent. For the first time, I heard my name echoing from the campus walls, giving me goosebumps. At that moment, I was blank, not knowing how the meeting would unfold. I slowly climbed the stairs, which felt like the longest yet and landed in the foyer of the boardroom. An assistant opened the door to the boardroom, and a dozen officials at the table stared at me with my name echoing in the background as the slogans got louder. Though we cordially exchanged greetings, the tone started to change much faster than me taking the seat at the center of the small side of the table.

"What nonsense is going on at the campus?" Questions from the adjacent side of the table thudded my ears.

"Sir, my only intention was to find the truth by engaging in questions and deep thinking about the subjects in the discussion."

"Who do you think you are?" One of the panelists said in a raised voice.

"Sir, I am no one; I am not for any chaos; rather, I want both those for and against the dialogue and questionnaire to live peacefully side by side on campus."

"You must be daydreaming; how can the opposing sides be peaceful?"

"Sir, those who want the dialogue and the debate could continue to assemble separately after the lectures?"

"Now you are telling us what to do? You know what? You should pack up and exit the campus."

The temperature was steadily rising in the room, and my eyelids started folding like a touch-me-not plant, fearing the worst may come true. Before my eyes turned to the ground, my gaze fell on a calm and composed face at the opposite end of the table, and he looked like he had authority in his appearance.

"I am the Vice Chancellor of the University. I know you are Dhaval and selling books at the campus, but I want to know more about you and your intentions," his low voice brought some calmness and coolness to the conference table as all panelists now looked at each other, giving me some confidence to respond.

"Thank you, sir, for giving me an opportunity. I lost my mother in a car accident when I was a child and have had head trauma for many years. My father and aunt home-schooled me because of my condition. This allowed me to read many books my mother used to read, such as Plato, Aristotle, Shakespeare, and many other historical books. I developed a passion for reading, writing, and poetry. My reading continued when I formally joined high school though I was isolated at school because of my condition. Yet I focused on my passion, but my father wanted me to study business at a university after my twelfth grade and take over the business empire he owned. Then the moment came when I fell in love with a girl of a different caste in the neighborhood, and my father used his caste and position to separate us when we decided to run away from home. And in that sightless running away, I got caught in those great floods of Mangalore, which washed away everything, including me, away from my father and home, and I lost everything I had loved. I never wanted to return to my father, and I discontinued my university studies without funding from him, though I had secured an offer to study literature at a prestigious university. Since then, I have searched for the truth in the world and of my life. I worked as a tea seller in trains and joined an ashram, yet nothing changed, but the stint at this university has given me a new direction to look forward to finding the truth."

"We know now how and why these things are happening on the campus; you can leave now and go away from the campus till we let you know our next step," though his voice had some sort of assurance that the decision would favor me, yet I left the room in confusion not knowing what my next turn of life would be.

# CHAPTER 47 WAITING

Student leaders came running to me when they sighted me down the stairs. I explained to them that the meeting went well, the Chancellor looked assured of my response, and they should go back to the classes without creating any noise on the campus by being friendly with the opposing students and waiting for the leadership's directions. My assurance made them step back from their aggressiveness as if I had some divine power to convince them, which greatly surprised me.

I went to my bookshop, picked up some of the new spiritual second-hand books, and went to my accommodation. Now I had time for myself though I was anxious for the next step in my life. I spent much time meditating with breathing patterns and mantras and read many books on spirituality and meditation.

Now away from daily routines of bookselling and debates, I started noticing subtle shifts in my life. My sense of self and the world had expanded a great deal. It seemed the world was much more vivid. Things became more apparent, and my perceptions were more defined. I saw color more profoundly. I saw the world differently than before. Things became alive, not just in my eyes, but in the essence of things. The details became more apparent. Things like black shadows were white, where the light is shaded, not just white or light, but in its color, little things that usually escape our vision. I started asking more questions and looking for more answers. For the answers seemed always to be there. Sometimes I would sit and listen and hear a response. A great many answers, sometimes as many as ten in a second. Sometimes as few as one. I started drinking liters of water daily and fasted from food, sometimes for twelve hours, sometimes twenty-four hours, and occasionally up to seventy-two hours. I started eating a lot of fruit and vegetables. As a result, I could taste more flavors. My mind was more precise and more energetic.

My heart began working as if it was in tune with everything else. Now I could feel when there was a change in the air, whether the air was cold or hot. I felt it in the way my whole body and mind responded. The wind could be calm and still, and I could sense it. A breeze was a breeze. Whether it was a gentle summer breeze or a heavy, cold storm blowing, it was still the same. I could feel the earth shifting and my heart pulse, almost as if it was a drum inside of me. I could feel the world respond.

I went through a phase of re-centering myself. I took long walks, every time not knowing where I was going.

In between my walks, I stood in empty fields and tried to understand the moments of life. Life was not always a struggle for victory. Sometimes, you have to accept the defeat and try to turn it into a learning moment. There were still days when I thought I couldn't do it. There were still days when I wanted to give up. I was struggling to adjust to everything that was happening around me. I couldn't eat. I couldn't sleep. I had been so concerned with my life that I lost my perspective of myself and my health.

I took up meditation more intensely. I started wearing simple clothes with no logos, brands, or colors, wanting my clothes to help me manifest my own better self. I started walking more regularly, often by a small water body. Suddenly I felt I was so incredibly healthy. And I was peaceful. One day, I woke up and just knew something wasn't right. It wasn't anything particular, just a general feeling that I had been disconnected for a long time, and the longer I went without being honest, the less I felt connected.

At night my mind was beset by feverish dreams, and I often felt high on drugs while entirely sober. I grew a shaggy beard and, some days rarely ventured out of the house. When I finally brought myself to eat again, I ate very little, but nothing processed or sugared, primarily fresh fruit and vegetables.

I became, almost overnight, a minimalist devoting myself to a life of intention and simplicity. No more would I allow myself to get attached to things, I told myself, for the things I became attached to all seemed to leave me. I wanted to empty my heart. I tried to open my mind, my body, and my soul. I wanted the self I knew to die. And a new self to be born.

# CHAPTER 48 NEW LIFE

A new dawn and day blossomed for me in a few weeks. The university called me to return to the campus, this time not to sell the books but to resume my university studies. I didn't know how this sudden change of direction occurred; perhaps students missed something that inspired them and made them think out of the box almost daily. Maybe the student leaders who supported me had their influence on the university management. Perhaps the Vice Chancellor saw something that the other management leaders didn't; maybe he thought this was the new direction the university should move forward. Perhaps he, too, wanted to find an absolute truth that would light the university and students alike.

With hugs and cheers, my friends and student leaders at the university welcomed me. I was made to feel how much they missed me, and I was happy to be among my friends who supported and stood by me in those days of confusion. There were no signs of opposition, and I wondered what made the environment change quickly, but I didn't want to know the reason anymore. When we get better or healed from sickness, we want to live in that moment and not look back at the struggles but learn how we got better or healed. I only wanted to look forward and no more back and learn from all situations. Meditation, mantras, and yoga have helped me to live in the moment.

Everything fell to the script as if I were an influential or very important person. I was helped by all staff and officers at the university office to enroll in my desired subjects of literature, philosophy, and psychology. I was told that the Vice Chancellor funded my entire stay and studies at the university. I couldn't believe how things were unfolding in front of me, and I thanked the Vice Chancellor when I had the opportunity to meet him for his belief in what I spoke in that meeting and for his great help in funding my studies. I promised him that I would put in all my efforts, now free from all kinds of work and distractions, to find the absolute truth of life.

I never felt so good in life until then, apart from my childhood when my mother was around. Now I had everything to smile about, and I started smiling within and outside. My voice and sight soothed the people and environment around me, and a light shined around the campus like a floodlight-lit stadium to focus on the action-packed sports event at the center. I felt like every cell of my body tuned in to focus on the task at hand, unearth the truth by studying and discerning the volumes of books of literature, philosophy, and psychology, and understanding the creation. The universe, various science, social, political, and theological exploration and thought processes from ancient to modern civilizations, and the world living then and now.

The entire university started buzzing with activities, debates, dialogues, and questionnaires, expressing and contradicting different views and thought processes during every subject's lecture. Students analyzed experiments, the writer's teachings, ideas, and their circumstances. They came up with their own opinions and took their stand boldly for and against the investigations, theories and philosophies, putting forward modified or new experiments and ideas, providing a new and exciting environment for everyone to progress in their development.

In a few months, weekend debates and dialogues resurfaced again, but this time the entire university took part in it at the university auditorium housing thousands of students. It was well organized with the best moderators of the university, live telecasted on social media, and attended by all the senior management, lecturers, and well-known local experts in their fields as judges. Then the best topic and debaters were selected every month based on attendees' and judges' voting. Once a month, the chosen debate and dialogue were organized at the city's town hall, attended by the public, other university students, and eminent personalities from all walks of life. As the noise and amazement got louder, the business houses advertised these events, and prominent TV channels live telecasted it to the length and breadth of the country, becoming one of the most sought-after current affairs shows. Every month the town hall and its surroundings bore the festive atmosphere, with the public and students attentively taking part in debates and dialogues the entire day. The food, the culture, the diversity, and the socialization further enriched these events making everyone, including me, eagerly wait for such events every month to learn and understand all aspects of life and the hidden truth behind those moments of life.

Each year I progressed well in the university with my close friends Bala, Navya, and Manal, studying different literature, philosophies, and psychological theories. In the evenings, we sat together and debated and discussed each subject and lecture, developing our ideas and questionnaires with intriguing analyses and analogies. At the year-end, we presented new theories and metaphors with dialogues at the university and then at the town hall to the applause of the mesmerized audience. These dialogues, which were live telecasted on TV channels, went viral on social media, with people commenting and posting their views and stories.

The university steadily climbed the ladder, becoming one of the top-ranked universities. There was a mad rush from every corner of the nation for enrollment, and Vice Chancellor and university management commended and awarded our performances. The university's social media handles were followed by millions of students and the public, evolving social and developmental movements. Our university created partnerships with other schools and universities, sharing and developing similar programs. Inter-university dialogues and debates brought out the best in the students for the development of society and the nation.

Vice Chancellor was proud about his vision coming true in front of his eyes. Yet I was far from finding the truth of life though I was sure these dialogues were in the right direction.

# CHAPTER 49 CREATION

I said, "Now let me show you how wonderful the creation is. Everything existed before our birth, the galaxy, the sun, the moon, the earth, oceans, animals, birds, all the trees, plants, and fruits. And then there were different animals, birds, vegetables, and fruits, and we named them as cow, tiger, nightingale, apple, palm tree, rocks, and so on. But for the universe, all these existed before we named them; they were all one creation, united with the power of creation. When a tree grows tall and spreads its branches, giving shape to the houses and furniture; when fruit trees flower and bear fruits giving us taste and energy; when flowering shrubs grow and blossom with flowers delighting our senses; when animals grow and reproduce, they all give glory to the creation, magnifying beauty, and purpose of creation."

**Bala**: That is true if we think deeper.

**Dhaval**: Like the trees, animals and shrubs have their purpose, we human beings, too, have a purpose in our life.

**Navya**: Certainly.

**Dhaval**: And now we have multi-billion people living in the world and an estimate that more than a hundred billion people lived and died. Yet not a single fingerprint of one human match another, not even twins!

**Manal**: True.

**Dhaval**: And our thinking, reactions, responses, emotions, and feelings for the same or similar situations are different?

**Bala**: Sure.

**Dhaval**: Then our passion, instincts, appearance, voice, desires, and goals are different?

**Manal**: Indeed.

**Dhaval**: And now let me tell you about human creation; cars, mobiles, televisions, furniture, and computers all have different purposes.

**Bala**: Certainly.

**Dhaval**: All creation, whether it is universal creation or human creation, nothing has been created or exists without any purpose. Look at these chairs we are sitting on now; they wouldn't be here if we could not sit on them.

**Navya**: No question.

**Dhaval**: And now there are different purposes within those creations. Toyota, Nissan, Mazda, Mercedes, and Ford are all different from each other, though they do the same thing – to take us from one place to another. Similarly, mobile phones, computers, and televisions of different specifications have different purposes.

**Bala**: I suppose.

**Dhaval**: But when these creations of human origin perform their purposes, aren't we happy that they did their goals and elevated the creator? Similarly, once we achieve our purposes, we glorify the universal creation.

**Manal**: Possibly.

**Dhaval**: Every creation needs to be obedient and connected to the creator. Otherwise, the free-flowing energy from the creator wouldn't pass to the creation, and it will suffer.

**Navya**: No question.

**Dhaval**: Once the creation starts doing its purpose, we see progress by creating new models of mobiles, cars, televisions, and so on. Similarly, once we start living our purpose, we will see improvement in our lives and in the universe; new talent, new thinking, new ways, and peace and harmony, glorifying creation. But if we didn't achieve our individual and collective purposes, there would be a disorder, and there wouldn't be much progress in the universe. The chaos and confusion would rule both our life and the world.

**Bala**: I see.

**Dhaval**: As all organs and parts belong to one body and all parts and organs have specific functions and purposes; there is one creation, and all belong to one universe, and everything has its purposes.

**Manal**: Good analogy.

**Dhaval**: Now let me show you why every creation has a purpose. Nothing can exist in this world by itself without a creator. All things, whether universal or human origin, cannot come into existence by themselves because the self cannot create itself. Since every creation has a source, the creator made it for a purpose. Like humans created vehicles for faster mobility, televisions, and mobile phones for entrainment and quicker communication, we exist for a purpose. Our purpose is to experience and explore the gigantic creation and glorify the creator.

**Navya**: That is interesting.

**Dhaval**: We have explored the creation since human existence step by step and not at once because it is a gigantic creation beyond our imagination. Over the years, we have discovered a solar system, the earth revolves around the sun, each of us has different fingerprints, and the list is endless. We have named every animal, tree, plant, and shrub. And we still find many new things daily. Science and scientists call it research; however, all these researched things or phenomena existed before someone found out.

**Manal**: Story within a story?

**Dhaval**: Every creator wants their product or creation to fulfill its purpose and, through those creations, wants to receive glory.

**Navya**: I suppose.

**Dhaval**: On the lighter side, humans take credit and glory for researching and finding what was created and existed before without giving credit to the creator.

**Bala**: That is a reality.

# CHAPTER 50 GOLDEN LIFE

"Let me now show you what life is all about. It is a journey for certain years, but we do not have control over the beginning of that journey nor know when that journey ends. Neither do we have control over where we begin, what environment we start living, or what would be our birth religion because we are not given a choice to choose our parents."

**Navya**: True.

**Dhaval**: Neither we have control over our birth intelligence, the color of our skin, our height, appearance, and passions when we grow up, but most of them are genetically transferred to us from our parents.

**Bala**: Certainly.

**Dhaval**: Though we have control over our life journey from birth to death, life is a process with different stages that no one can bypass. It takes five to six years to start going to primary school, sixteen to eighteen years old to become legal adults, then study, work, marry, have kids, and juggle life till we retire at around sixty years. Yet most of us seem lost in regrets, in ifs and buts, and not content in life even though we have gone through the universal life processes and are closing in on our end point of the journey!

**Navya**: Feels to be accurate, but why so?

**Dhaval**: What would happen if we don't connect our smart phone to the internet and manufacturer? We wouldn't be able to update the apps now and then, lessening some of its capabilities, and over some time, we may not be able to use the phone as efficiently or struggle to operate it. Similarly, if we don't connect to our creator or power beyond, we may not get the inspirations and energy to live life to the fullest and to our satisfaction.

**Manal**: Interesting analogy, but how do we connect to our creator?

**Dhaval**: By meditation, prayer, loving creator, self and others, sharing and caring, by being in communion with people around us and with nature. By feeling the breeze on our faces when we go for a walk and happy seeing the shrubs and trees bearing flowers and fruits. By feeling delightful witnessing the sunset and sunrise; seeing the sky— sometimes clear and sometimes cloudy; by seeing the lightening and experiencing the rain and thunders; by watching the magnitude of solar and lunar eclipses, listening to music, watching the sports and cinema we like, by visiting the places of worship and helping the needy and so on.

**Bala**: Interesting, but isn't it difficult to have positive feelings and happiness all the time?

**Dhaval**: When we live in the current moment all the time, and by not regretting the past and not worrying about the future, we can develop a grateful heart, feeling happy about all the moments of our life.

**Navya**: Can we be happy in our suffering and tragedies?

**Dhaval**: Of course not! It is, again, a process of life. Suffering, tragedies, and demanding situations are part of life. For some, life is full of sorrow; for others, it may be lesser, but all would have to go through these suffering processes one way or another. It is like gold going through the fire for it to shine, like an athlete going through everyday practice with pain and sweat to win the championship. The pain and sweat of our suffering would ultimately crown our life by making us understand what life is all about. And loving, sharing, and caring in those difficult moments would make us realize our life's purpose and give us patience and perseverance to live in that purpose.

**Bala:** Good analogy of gold and athlete, but it is hard to comprehend.

**Dhaval:** Our struggles are authentic, and we all go through unique situations; some are comparable with others, but life can be full of broken relationships and struggles. But suppose we persevere in those moments, sticking to the basics of life such as patience, love, gratitude, sharing, and caring in communion. In that case, victory is ours, with the ultimate crown full of joy, happiness, and contentment.

**Bala:** This is very hard, but what about tragedies and loss?

**Dhaval:** Once again, tragedies and losses are part of life, and we should go through grief and loss because we have feelings and emotions as humans. Though most of the time, we do not have these events in our control, we should remember that we are all temporary in this world. We have come into this world without anything and will go back from this world without taking anything. Therefore, we mustn't attach to anything in this world, whether it is people around us, materials, or desires. Otherwise, it would be difficult to escape from our grief and loss. I was so attached to my mother. When she died in a car accident, I went into a shell, and it took years for me to come out!

**Navya:** Isn’t life hard, then?

**Dhaval**: There is a purpose even in such situations. If not, I wouldn't have been here working hard to know the truth. Now I understand that love is the corner stone of the entire creation and absolute truth sustains and progresses the creation to attain its ultimate glory. Therefore, living in all situations and circumstances becomes wonderful only if we understand our purpose in this gigantic world and live life to the best of our abilities, no matter the situation.

**Bala**: How can we understand our purpose?

**Dhaval**: By connecting to our creator. An open, receptive and current mind is also a prerequisite for knowing our purpose. Only the creator knows our purpose. In the human creation of cars and smart phones, only the creator knows for what purpose these have been created and what specifications and characteristics they require for their purpose.

**Manal**: Interesting analogy, but true.

**Dhaval**: Everything has a purpose, and we inflict misery upon ourselves by not carrying out our purpose. Everything has a creator or force, as nothing can be in existence by itself. Amid our hard work, we will have joy and happiness if we connect with our creator. Ultimate joy and happiness can only come to us through our creator. If I am happy, I will always see happy people around me; if I am sad, I always see unhappy people around me.

**Navya**: I suppose.

**Dhaval**: When we acknowledge our creator and connect with the creator, there will be order, system, and righteousness. If we do not attach to the creator, there won't be truth and justice because we wouldn't have the attributes of the creator. Like the major repairs of any cars or gadgets done by the manufacturer, we too ought to be corrected by our creator if we are on the wrong path from our purpose. The connection with our creator will return us to the correct pathway to complete our incredible life journey.

**Bala**: That is interesting, but what if one loses one's life amid suffering and struggles?

**Dhaval**: Even in death, there would be a shining light just like a seed dies for it to sprout and bring a new life. How many freedom fighters and saints have been killed in their struggle for freedom, truth, and oppression? Their death brought light upon people and the nation around them. They persevered and rejoiced in their suffering; today, we have freedom and truth because of their struggles and martyrdom.

**Navya**: Wow, indeed, life is wonderful if we live our purpose connecting to our creator, to live a golden life!

# CHAPTER 51 WORLD ORDER

"Now let me show you why and how we are struggling in this wonderfully created world, the home for our life journey by the three great greeds of humankind; greed for wealth, power, and sex. The moreism desire of every aspect of our life somehow makes us forget that our journey is temporary in this world and makes us run behind to accumulate more and more without questioning how much we need or why we need it."

**Manal**: Interesting observation.

**Dhaval**: Greed makes us fear losing our possessions or feel that what we have may not be enough, and we accumulate or desire more. Then we get so obsessed that we lose control over ourselves and become the slave of these selfish possessions and desires.

**Navya**: Certainly.

**Dhaval**: Once we lose control over ourselves, we try to become wealthier or more powerful or desire more sex or change sex partners now and then. Our eyes, minds, and hearts become indifferent to the world and people around us as we go after our selfish goals and desires.

**Bala**: No question.

**Dhaval**: These indifferences bring psychological blindness as we become fearful of losing our acquired hold on wealth or power or sexual desires, developing our pride and arrogance and lessening in us the human virtue of humility, kindness, empathy, generosity, and love for the neighbor.

**Manal**: I suppose.

**Dhaval**: When the blindness covers the wealthy and powerful with layers of masks, they feel they are gods, powerful and invincible, having all knowledge and wisdom and could do no wrong. They expect all to worship, praise, and follow them. They wouldn't tolerate criticism, competition, opposition, and challengers and become numb to the world outside their own and their advisors and followers.

**Bala**: Interesting observations and I can already put these attributes to many past and current leaders.

**Dhaval**: They get so much attached to their power and wealth; they hardly trust anyone other than their closest circle. They feel there wouldn't be anyone matching their intelligence, capacity, and capability to run their show or to do what they are doing. They will go to any extent to eliminate their challengers, hold on to their position, and not share or give the opportunity to others.

**Navya**: Certainly.

**Dhaval**: This absolute power corrupts them and their followers, waging ideological and physical conflicts over their opponents, such as wars, excessive nationalism, stifling and arresting opposition, and instigating violence. This brings the destruction of innocents and opposition in the world around them, ultimately leading to their downfall and destruction.

**Manal**: I can relate this to World War II and many other conflicts in many countries and continents.

**Dhaval**: Holding on to anything, whether it is wealth or power or worldly desires beyond one's need and purpose in life and not giving an opportunity to others stagnates one's life and the development of the world and exploration of creation by running out of ideas. Similarly, not playing one's role in this gigantic glory of creation would also bear the same consequences.

**Manal**: I suppose all should play their roles to near perfection.

**Dhaval**: Absolutely. Consider team sports like soccer, where players play different roles such as forward, midfielder, defender, and goalkeeper, or cricket, where batters, bowlers, and fielders play different roles at different moments to become victorious. Then we see teams changing captains after some time because no sportsperson is invincible as they run out of ideas or inspiration for the teams to win the matches and championships. Yet, after relinquishing leadership, they still play as a team member and help win the games.

**Navya**: No question.

**Dhaval**: New ideas, inspiration, and ways flow when captains change and the team starts winning. We require a similar approach in all fields of the world, be it political, religious, or business. Every area requires new leadership and new team players now and then for new talent to blossom. This would inspire holistic, continuous development in all fields, instilling peace in the world. All leaders and team players are different and unique and have specific in-built talent, perspective, inspirations, and thought processes. Each look at situations differently, and when they play their role to perfection in their given time, we will have a new world, dwelling in peace and glorifying creation.

**Bala**: Indeed, that would be something glorious.

# CHAPTER 52
# CONSEQUENCES

"Why do we have global warming? If you research, you will find that electrical technology for vehicles came before oil technology. However, oil technology quickly promoted some countries' petro economy and money power. Therefore, electrical technology was completely neglected until recently. Global warming is the consequence of overusing fossil fuels, posing dire threats to climate change and environmental pollution. If global warming is not tackled properly, we may end up losing many low-laying islands and inflicting severe sicknesses to children, striking a big blow to the healthy living conditions for future generations."

**Bala**: Genuine and scary situation.

**Dhaval**: Everything we do and act in our life journey as individuals or as a group in this world have either rewards or consequences for us and the world around us. If we work or carry out anything selflessly, there will be rewards, and if we act and carry out anything selfishly, there will be consequences. Newton's third law, 'every action reacts,' also holds good to everything we do.

**Manal**: I suppose.

**Dhaval**: Rewards or consequences are directly proportional to the authority one holds. If an ordinary person does his work with a selfish motive, the results would be for him and the people around him at his home, neighborhood, and workplace. If a president, prime minister, or business leader enforces decisions with selfish motives, the consequences will be for their nation and the entire world.

**Navya**: Certainly.

**Dhaval**: The world is facing the consequences of wars and politically supported violence, terrorism, religious fundamentalism, caste, and race intolerance due to the selfish goals of the leaders to remain in power or grab more power and wealth. The selfishness of a few people can force family violence and neighborhood disharmony.

**Bala**: True, but why do we act selfishly?

**Dhaval**: To gain or hold on status, power, and wealth over others. If leaders do not have or develop the virtue of humility and humbleness, then power and wealth corrupts them, enslaving them. This makes them control everything through the eyes of power, wealth, and money; inflicting misery on the people and the world.

**Manal**: No question.

**Dhaval**: Rather, money, wealth, and power should follow us, becoming our slaves, and we would become masters to control these enslaved desires as we want.

**Navya**: That could be very hard for most people.

**Dhaval**: Certainly tricky, but if not in control, it spreads like cancer. Once we start doing small things through the eyes of money, wealth, and power, it spreads like wildfire. Then we start doing everything, small or big, to gain wealth and power. We would always calculate how much we would earn by doing certain things and may not act if we wouldn't gain something.

**Bala:** Very true.

**Dhaval:** This cancer then spreads like a virus to the followers of these corrupt leaders, misusing their power and position and bringing chaos to the poor and vulnerable.

**Manal:** Indeed.

**Dhaval:** We know how difficult it is to survive if we don't treat cancer in the early stage. Similarly, suppose we don't treat the corruption and misuse of power. In that case, the entire state becomes cancerous in corruption and injustice, halting the growth and development of the nation and brining misery to ordinary people.

**Navya:** We are indeed experiencing the effects of such cancerous corruption in everyday life.

**Dhaval:** If we don't act selflessly on time with good intentions, it has consequences like global warming. Even after experiencing these consequences, we are yet to work purposefully as the situation worsens daily. Similarly, wars and terrorism are consequences of not acting selflessly and on time with purpose. If we had acted on time, many wars, terrorism, and violence could have been avoided.

**Bala:** Very real, as we can draw on many parallels and experiences from history and the current world.

**Dhaval:** If there is a wound in our hand, it is not only the hand that pains, but the entire body is in discomfort. When we are mentally sick, it is not only the brain that is affected but the whole body. Similarly, the good and bad works or actions, selfish and selfless work or actions affect not only the person or group of people who carry it out, but also the people around them, and the entire world.

**Manal:** Certainly. The entire world is affected and is in chaos by the evil and selfish actions of a few. On the other hand, the world has progressed because of the reasonable efforts of leaders such as Mahatma Gandhi and Martin Luther King Jr., to name a few. Many scientific inventions such as communications, flying, electricity and the advancement of medical technology and medicines have hugely benefitted humanity and the world's progress.

# CHAPTER 53 RELIGION

"One of the freedoms we need today is from religious fundamentalism. Religion is human-made, and some religions are human responses to God's initiative, whereas others are born out of a human desire to find God. However, political and religious leaders have used and are using religion to gain and hold on to power and oppress people in the name of religion, developing conflicts throughout human history and in the current world."

**Navya**: Agree, but without religion, how can humans exist, and how do we build our connection to the creator?

**Dhaval**: Of course, we need religion and freedom from religious fundamentalism simultaneously. Most religions believe there is only one God, and religion is the pathway to God. Therefore, different religions form many ways, and every human should be given a choice to choose and practice their religion or paths.

**Manal**: Interesting, but how?

**Dhaval**: We need liberalization of religion as we have done with economic liberalization in many countries. Faith was made for humans, not humans for religion. We should decontrol religion from religious and political leaders and allow people to choose their best pathway to connect with the creator.

**Bala**: Certainly; however, how to enlighten the fundamentalists?

**Dhaval**: We have been given the freedom to choose our daily use products such as cars, mobile phones, televisions, soaps, food, clothes, and restaurants, etc., and we freely select the products and brands in this age of the internet by seeing the advertisements, reviews, experiences and then trying it out ourselves. Everyone does not buy the same product or force others to buy a particular brand. People choose their products based on their requirements and the product's suitability to meet those requirements. Many of us change our product brands over time, sometimes new products, styles, and cuisines. Similarly, people should be allowed to choose their religion, the pathway that best suits them, without force or threats.

**Manal**: But how to enlighten the leaders who control the religion and force on people their authority?

**Dhaval**: Like mechanics are trained to serve the connection between the creator (for example, Mercedes, Apple) and creation (Mercedes cars, Apple products); religious leaders, the gurus, and the priests should serve the creation and facilitate the connection between creator and creation. Control should be between the creator and creation and not by a third party (mechanic or the priest).

**Navya**: Fascinating analogy.

**Dhaval**: First, religious leaders' tenure in their position of power should be limited, ideally three years but not more than five years. This will help to lessen the greed for power and people following them as gods. Then, new talent will rise with inspiration, and ways of newness will motivate people on their paths to the creator.

**Bala**: Indeed, but who will bell the cat?

**Dhaval**: As Gandhi said, "be the change you want to see in the world." As we change ourselves by walking the talk, the world around us will change, and nature will bring about those changes through its divine power. Remember, divine power is always ahead of us; we need to do only what we need to do.

**Manal**: But how would people know what is best for them?

**Dhaval**: We need to throw open all religions to all the people. Like the advertisers use models to convey their message and experiences, religions should use their role models who walk the talk and live the best life in their faith with peace, love, sharing, and caring. Indeed there is no place for any violence or hatred in any religion. Throw open all the literature and sacred scriptures of all faiths to all people, especially students in colleges and universities, to bring them to the truth that there is only one God, many pathways and entire creation shall come together to live the abundant life."

**Navya**: Interesting and unique.

**Dhaval**: Those who want others to follow their religion should be the role models of peace, selfless love, and charity so that those who wish to follow them are inspired to walk their pathways.

**Bala**: True.

**Dhaval**: Most people got their religion from their parents when they had no control over selecting their parents. Therefore, it is unjustifiable to blame them for their religious beliefs. But it is essential to provide the pathways and truth by giving the opportunity of education to gain knowledge for everyone in the world. This will help to eradicate the religion of violence and intolerance and the army of fundamentalists from all religions; as people would choose the religion of peace, love, harmony, sharing, and caring.

**Navya**: Certainly, this would give freedom from religious fundamentalism for a peaceful and caring world.

**Dhaval**: Whatever our religion, it should only be in our hearts and not on our sleeves, allowing us to go out and serve everyone around us by divine power without judging others' religions, caste, status, and color. Then the people would not fight for a particular religion, and there wouldn't be any power games, but all would be equal. All would have peace and freedom to choose their faith and live their life to the fullest.

**Manal**: That would be amazing.

**Dhaval**: Bringing people from different religions and all walks of life together to celebrate life and worship the creator in their traditions and ceremonies, while respecting each other's faith and protocols would add the icing on the cake.

**Bala**: That would indeed be out of this world.

# CHAPTER 54 SOCIETY AND THE WORLD

"Family is the nucleus of the society, and society is the nucleus of the country, and the country is the nucleus of the world. Suppose every family in society is healthy. In that case, society becomes healthy, and if every society is healthy, the country becomes healthy. If every country in the world is healthy, then the world will become healthy and prosperous."

**Manal**: No question.

**Dhaval**: Now, let me ask you if our hand gets a cut or an injury or, for that matter, any organ or part of the body gets an injury, does it pain only the hand or that part or organ of the body or discomforts the entire body as well?

**Navya**: Certainly, the entire body would be in discomfort no matter which part or organ has an injury.

**Dhaval**: Similarly, even if one family member is sick or not doing their purpose in life, the entire family suffers and is in discomfort. The same is true for society. The community would be uncomfortable if one family didn't live life to the fullest in peace, love, and joy. Even if one society does not live in peace and harmony with another, the country will suffer, and even if one country doesn't live in freedom and peace, the entire world will be in discomfort.

**Manal:** True. Now we know why there is no peace in most countries and the world.

**Dhaval:** Our muscle memory in our childhood captures all that happens at home. If there were violence, hatred, unhappiness, and brokenness, the children would portray the intolerance and disgust around them as they grow up. We would reap what we sow, impacting the progress of societies and nations.

**Navya:** Home is such an important place in everybody's life and plays a vital role in our nurture.

**Dhaval:** Certainly. If the home is the nucleus, then society is the eye of the nation. The diversity and unity of society are essential to celebrate life and creation glory. Like we can't eat the same food or watch the same movie every day, we are all diverse but should be united for the creation glory to spread peace, love, joy, and abundant living.

**Manal:** Peaceful societies are mirrors of the nation!

**Dhaval:** Absolutely. We can unite all societies by celebrating neighbor's day, all festivals of all religions by all people, and glorifying the great work of all people. Celebrating talent and success and sharing struggles, difficulties, and sickness would bring together all neighborhoods and societies to create open communities to know each other and to live happily, sharing and caring.

**Bala:** That would be celebrating every day of our life.

**Dhaval:** Indeed. We all can celebrate our life if we treat the discomforts of our families and societies in due time like we treat our sicknesses the moment we get sick. They may aggravate if we don't treat some of our sicknesses at the right time. Similarly, if we don't put our efforts into bringing peace and harmony in our families, society, and nation, the situation may worsen, severely affecting the community and country.

**Manal**: It is like cancer; if we don't detect and treat it early enough, it may spread and consume us.

**Dhaval**: Surely. It is like how we cannot live our everyday life comfortably and make any progress when we are sick with incurable diseases. Similarly, the society and nation wouldn't be able to live in peace and achieve progress if we don't treat and heal the ills such as hatred, intolerance, corruption, pride and arrogance, and so on.

**Navya**: True, that is why many nations cannot make progress because of their corruption, pride, intolerance, and arrogance of the leaders and hatred among different groups of religion, caste, language, and states.

**Dhaval**: It is like how our body reacts when a virus attacks, producing antigens that may harm our immune system. Similarly, nature or the universe responds when leaders and people live and act selfishly by greed for power and wealth, corruption, and hatred, curtailing the progress that was made in the world.

**Manal**: Indeed, nature or the universe reacts differently, such as global warming, floods, drought, pandemics, wildfires, etc.

**Dhaval**: Like our body's immune system, the world sometimes attacks us like an autoimmune disease, though we wouldn't know the reason, and sometimes it repels back, harming us significantly.

**Navya**: No question.

**Dhaval**: Like a serious wound or sickness lugs more pain for that organ and body; greater hatred, corruption, greed, and pride promote more disharmony and disorientation in the society and nation, affecting the entire world.

**Manal**: Ture, and because of today's global connectivity, the ills are not limited to specific nations or continents. They quickly spread throughout the world like a pandemic.

# CHAPTER 55 LEADERSHIP AND THE WORLD

"It is leaders and their good work and actions that are instrumental for the stability and progress of the world. A leader with selfish motives, greed for power, pride, and arrogance destroys their nation, the entire world, and its progress. A selfless leader unites and serves all people without any barrier to religion, caste, and creed for the progress of their nation and the world. On the other hand, the authoritative leaders divide the people of their nation by their caste, religion, and status to gain or hold on to power without much progress for the entire nation."

**Bala**: Certainly, all the wars and violence in the world in the past and present are due to the selfishness of a few leaders.

**Dhaval**: Absolutely. If the intentions of the leaders and their followers are not selfless, it would ultimately bring disharmony and pain to the society and nation and then to the entire world.

**Manal**: I suppose the leaders have to show the way.

**Dhaval**: Rightly said. But leaders and followers should be sensitive to each other; followers shouldn't put their leaders on the pedestal or throne, and leaders shouldn't allow their followers to follow them blindly, rather be the critique of their excellent and not-so-good work.

**Navya**: That would be something not heard of in the current world.

**Dhaval**: Very much, but for the authoritative and mass leaders, their blind followers would be a more significant threat than their enemies. If the followers follow them blindly, the leaders might think they are invincible on all fronts, building more pride and arrogance in them. At the same time, the followers may rampage when the leaders lose the election or public confidence.

**Bala**: Indeed, the blind followers of authoritative leaders carry a serious threat to the leaders, society, and country. We have seen many riots carried out to support their leaders, resulting in loss of life and public property.

**Dhaval**: Therefore, leaders should have complete humility, put themselves last among fellow citizens and reduce themselves to zero, as Gandhi said.

**Navya**: They should have a selfless dream like Martin Luther King Jr.

**Dhaval**: Certainly, leaders can only have dreams when they become selfless and serve the people with humility without expecting anything in return. Therefore, political and religious leaders should volunteer their work rather than take it as a career or profession.

**Manal**: That would be a significant paradigm shift.

**Dhaval**: Ideally, they shouldn't occupy any position of power for more than five years, and more years in the position of power would bring selfishness, greed, attachment, pride, and arrogance.

**Bala**: It is a reality, but why?

**Dhaval**: At the beginning of civilization, there wasn't much education, and only the royal and wealthy had the opportunity to govern and rule, which continued with their descendants. But in today's world, most people are educated, and hence they can express their passion, inbuilt talent and capabilities, views, and inspirations uniquely. Therefore, it is essential to allow many people to become leaders for the continuous development and progress of the world through their different talents and motivations.

**Navya**: Wow, now many deserving people will get an opportunity to serve, and we can imagine the interest of people, especially youth, to participate in the political process to achieve progress for the people and the development of the nation and world around them.

**Dhaval**: Certainly. Many more people would be involved in choosing the right candidate to represent them. Parents and elders would come out and support such a process as they could dream for their children to serve them and the people around them. Every deserving and aspiring youth would get an opportunity to employ their talent and inspiration.

**Bala**: This will give new impetus to the entire system and people.

**Dhaval**: Look at the team sports and their captains. They change their captain once they start losing or after a few years, even though the captain still plays in the team. This creates renewal and new ideas. Allowing all deserving players to become leaders is essential so that we will have different inspirations, talents, views, and focus.

**Bala**: Fascinating analogy. The opportunity for deserving players to become leaders inspires the team to go ahead and perform well all the time.

**Dhaval**: We will see this world transform when we allow everyone to become leaders based on their talent and capabilities at the right time. This will help leaders to detach from their power and step down from their positions. This would bring new inspiration and innovation among the young and youth, who will come forward to serve the people, nation, and the world.

**Bala**: Certainly, a great way to transform the world.

**Dhaval**: Finally, the leaders need to serve all people without bias for religion, caste, and creed for the progress and development of the people, society, and country and the complete transformation of the world.

**Bala**: Then the caste, creed, religion, nationalism, and polarization will take a back seat, and humanity will unite for the progress of the entire world, glorifying the creation.

# CHAPTER 56 ECONOMY AND THE WORLD

"We live in an ever-changing world. While thousands of years ago, humans worked all by themselves, hunting and fashioning items to wear. They had just enough to fill their stomach, one of the very few basic needs of that time! Many lived in undivided families in huts built using naturally available tree trunks and hay and wore dresses made from naturally available leaves and animal skin. They danced, sang, created paintings and art, and played sports to entertain themselves. But as humans became civilized and increased in population, their basic needs widened to shelter, education, healthcare, and recreation. Families were divided until they became nuclear families what we see today, to afford better living!"

**Navya:** That is the evolution and civilization of the world!

**Dhaval:** True, and the evolution continued. With their growing needs, humans searched for one invention after another to find a better living. Every century saw new, life-changing, and ground-breaking discoveries like electricity, telephone, television, and industrial revolutions, making more human hands and bodies free of work.

**Bala**: That has led to the invention of technology which has made us connect the world at our fingertips, isn't it?

**Dhaval**: There are many good things about technology but some bad. Unfortunately, the same technology we like so much and can't live without has become more important than for whom it has been created! Some of us don't even know who our neighbor is or who is walking next to us in the street or at the road crossing, as we are so hooked on our smart devices! We have forgotten human touch and expressions! And slowly, we are losing the specialty of the human species' expressions of smiling, dancing, acting, singing, and sporting in many people!

**Manal**: Certainly! The localized dance/acting, singing/music, painting, art and craft, and sports entertainment were replaced mainly by movie theatres and televisions. Then the twentieth century's invention of computers, the internet, robots, and AI increased unemployment in today's world!

**Dhaval**: We need new technology and inventions, don't get me wrong. They are all beautiful things that happened to better human life over the years! Today we sit at home and do most of our work at the click of a button, like transferring money between accounts, buying groceries or dresses, and watching matches live. In contrast, our parents or grandparents took hours or days to do the same activities!

**Bala**: But the current era of free-market capitalism took advantage of technological progress to deprive the underdeveloped world of equality by imitating low wages in the developing world. And in a few years, all machines, including vehicles, will be operated or driven by computers and robots. We can imagine what will happen to employment then!

**Navya:** Every person in today's world should have enough to eat, have a primary education, a decent shelter, and access to healthcare no matter which country or part of the world we live in, and for that to happen, there should be enough employment available. But how can we do that?

**Dhaval:** One of the first efforts towards employing everyone is to educate everyone in this world. There are still millions of people around the globe who are illiterate! Remember, everyone has a unique inbuilt passion for their career, and without education and skill development, people can't get into the career they are passionate about.

**Manal:** The next major task is to have comparable minimum wages worldwide! The minimum wages are as high as USD 13.78 per hour in Luxembourg and less than one USD per hour in most Asian and African countries. What a grave injustice to humanity! The capitalist world has hugely benefitted from this injustice. It continues its nexus with the world's political leadership to gain wealth rather than vouching for equal wages and development worldwide!

**Bala:** The vast disparity in minimum wages has made corporations worldwide move their production and customer service units from high-wage to low-wage countries. This has resulted in the loss of jobs in high-wage countries, and though the low-wage countries have benefitted and the living conditions of the workers have improved, but nowhere near the ideal conditions. These conditions would stay at the bare minimum levels, as any efforts to increase the wages in the developing world comparable to the developed world would drive away the corporates and cause the poor laborers to remain poor for many generations!

**Dhaval:** If every country manufactures what it requires (demands), from mobile phones to toys, there will be a balance in the job market worldwide, and wages will be improved in the developing world. The giant corporates should be persuaded for the patented technologies to flow without borders between the countries with reasonable royalties. Then training in required skills and localized manufacturing of every goods will help develop the emerging countries to better their living standards!

**Navya**: The larger populated and geographically more extensive countries should further localize the production in every state and district. This would avoid the clogging of cities and develop the rural/regional economy, and it would also reduce environmental pollution by minimizing cargo movements worldwide.

**Manal**: Soon, automation (computers) and AI (artificial intelligence) will overtake most human jobs, and we should prepare new ways of employment from now onwards!

**Dhaval**: Of course, it is wonderful to advance in technology, helping us with better living conditions worldwide by eliminating diseases and poverty. At the same time, every person should find employment in the passion, talent, and profession/field they like, providing a sense of belonging and job satisfaction. As we know, each of us has a different built-in liking, and with education, one can understand our favored field of work! Automation and AI may be a blessing in disguise to pursue a career for everyone according to their passion and talent to enhance their well-being and the community around them!

**Bala**: We should focus on human expressions of dance/acting, singing/music, painting, art and craft, and sports to generate more employment when computers and AI cut most jobs. Every country has its traditional forms of various dances, music, paintings, and sports. When these diverse ranges of human expressions are promoted professionally, they all become employment sources.

**Navya**: Various sports leagues in different parts of the world are prime examples, whether in soccer, cricket, or tennis. They have created a good number of employment and have contributed immensely to the economy. Suppose these sports leagues are further developed to go deep down to the college/council/zonal level sporting culture. In that case, one can expect to generate hundreds of thousands of jobs by developing infrastructure, sports gear, training and fitness facilities, staff, etc.

**Manal**: Large movie industries like Hollywood and Bollywood are another example of promoting cinema and acting, creating employment, and contributing to the economy. Suppose movie industries can further develop theater, music, and cinema technology skills at colleges and zonal levels by developing the infrastructure, such as studios and technical and agility training. In that case, we can witness a new era of talent spotting and sound employment generation.

**Dhaval**: Great ideas! Similar models of sports leagues could be followed in dance and acting, singing and music, art, craft, and literature. Already shows such as Britain's Got Talent, American Idol, Master Chef, Indian Idol, and many other similar shows promote various talents in many different fields, successfully generating employment worldwide. If more such programs are promoted to the college/council/zonal level, it can develop more engagement and employment.

**Bala**: But would the rich and powerful, politics and business nexuses allow such development around the world for fear of losing control?

**Dhaval**: There is nothing wrong with being rich or powerful if that is the purpose of life. But if we hold on to wealth and power beyond one's requirements, it would stall the world's communion, sharing, and development. Money should follow us, and we should not follow money. Let's allow everyone an opportunity and educate people to use their talent and inbuilt capabilities. Then we will have a new world full of joy, sharing, caring, living abundantly, and celebrating life!

# CHAPTER 57 EDUCATION AND THE WORLD

"Only education can open up the minds of humans. The unique talent that everyone has to better this world can't be utilized unless everyone is educated. There are more than 700 million illiterate people in the world!"

**Manal**: That is a staggering number!

**Dhaval**: Yes, it is. Most of these people live in Africa and Asia. Illiteracy, unemployment, and poverty go hand in hand. When countries are poor, education opportunities are less, and even when available in rare, children are often forced to work in those developing countries to help struggling families. Some of the poorest countries in Africa and Asia have less than fifty percent literacy rates, and nearly two-thirds are female.

**Navya**: Even in the modern world, women are left far behind!

**Bala**: Yes, it seems like equality is only on paper, and it is time for us to force that change in reality. Remember, change begins with us.

**Dhaval**: Wow, that is a good intention, Bala. Remember, every new beginning starts with a positive intension. In reality, we need women in every field in equal numbers, and then only we can see the world's progress.

**Manal**: We also need to change the mind-set that women are traditionally homebound and men are office-bound.

**Dhaval**: The potential of everyone should be realized without gender bias or judgments and by providing an opportunity for all, starting with education. Education would give identity and purpose to all, bringing out the best in all, their passion, talent, skill development, different perspectives, and desire to find absolute truth. Remember, only truth can set us free!

**Navya**: Then why people who are responsible do not prioritize education?

**Dhaval**: That is a million-dollar question! I think responsible people do not want people to be educated faster and self-develop due to fear of losing their power and position. If people are educated and allowed to explore their talent and inbuilt capabilities, they would shape their future and vote out those who do not provide equal opportunities, unite and build the communities and nation.

**Bala**: Yet, well-educated people blindly follow some leaders who divide and rule worldwide?

**Manal**: That is a mystery to me as well. Perhaps we do not have selfless leaders beyond hyper-nationalism, caste, creed, and religion. Therefore people have to idolize someone, and they put mortal leaders on a pedestal who promote divide-and-rule policy, benefitting educated people on either side of the spectrum.

**Dhaval**: Imagine if all are allowed to educate and shape their future, then everyone would know how to feed and shelter themselves, stay healthy and climb the ladder of their life. Then they would reach the end of the earth with their talent, peace, harmony, and love to bind everything to celebrate life!

**Bala**: Wow, if all would be provided an opportunity for the right kind of education, such as moral, righteous, just, and harmonious education, and not just an education that shows the people how to be successful at any cost, then people would explore the truth beyond illusion. They would become the master of their own, finding all they need to live life in abundance, sharing, caring, and loving everyone around them.

**Dhaval**: You nailed it, Bala! Then people would know life is temporary on this planet, and they would make every effort to experience and celebrate life without holding on to more than what they require but only keeping what is necessary to live their temporary life wonderfully. Not holding on to power, wealth, and position beyond one's essential purpose and mission provides an opportunity for all to fulfill everyone's role and mission in this beautiful world, glorifying the magnanimous creation beyond our understanding.

**Manal**: The early education opportunity for everyone should focus on morals, ethics, harmony, peace, love, and respect for each other. The next level opportunity in education would help to explore one's passion and instincts and develop skills to utilize their passion and talent to the full extent, helping everyone to fulfill their great mission in the gigantic creation.

**Navya**: Learning and upskilling is a lifelong event, and all efforts should be made to provide practical and thought-provoking education in all fields that develop the human sciences and beyond, so that we can make significant progress to celebrate life in every moment.

**Bala**: So, the mantra should be then educate, educate and educate everyone, and we would have new ways and new direction to live and celebrate the life that is beyond the everyday living with attachments, sadness, loss, disappointments, suffering, disrespect, abuse, rapes, poverty, illiterate, shame and loneliness.

**Dhaval**: Absolutely. When provided unlimited opportunities to all to get educated in their fields of passion and inbuilt talent; a new world would be built, where all will have everything they need to celebrate life, remembering the world is made for humans and not humans are made for the world!

# CHAPTER 58 NEW WORLD

"A world for everyone to live freely, in any country or corner of the planet, doing whatever one wants, celebrating every moment of life, traveling, singing, dancing, and seeing the world from all directions, working in any field one is interested in, loving, caring, sharing, and respecting each other; living joyously in a communion exploring and glorifying creation."

**Bala**: Are we dreaming? Can that dream come true, perhaps at least on paper?

**Dhaval**: Of course, we are not just dreaming! Dreams are meant to be realized, aren't they? Suppose we practice humanity and its virtues of truth, righteousness, and justice and find selfless and righteous leaders to lead every nation without attachment to power, wealth, and position. In that case, we could have a peaceful and prosperous world. The world where every human would have all basic needs, and everyone would be allowed to fulfill their passion and purpose to explore, share, care, and better this world, every moment of their life, freely traveling around the world experiencing natural wonders and magnifying the creation glory!

**Navya**: Like every person is unique, every country has its traditions, history, and natural wonders! Just imagine everyone in this world travels around their country or internationally, experiences different cultures, history, and nature's wonders, and participates in different art, music, dance, sports, and cinema shows! This will change humanity and human expressions, always realizing and experiencing the wonders of this great planet and human creativity!

**Dhaval**: Absolutely, we are all so unique; every one of us has a special role in this gigantic creation. And the world will become dynamic when everyone plays that unique role with their fantastic talent and purpose. Otherwise, the world would move forward shakily, like a car moving wobbling when the air pressure is dropped and not equal in all tires.

**Manal**: At the moment, there are around one billion people who travel on holidays and for tourism in a calendar year around the world, and if the 7.7 billion people (current world population) have an opportunity to travel and explore the world, we would require seven times more infrastructure in airports, seaports, train stations, airplanes, trains, and vehicles. Then we would require many more travel agents, tour operators, tour guides, hotels, restaurants, etc.! It would be an astonishing number that would generate employment and empower humanity by seeing and experiencing beautiful creation glory!

**Bala**: How to get everyone to travel worldwide and promote the tourism economy?

**Dhaval**: For that, we need to end the war economy! The world spends more than 2 trillion dollars annually on military and defense equipment. Suppose we centralize the military and defense equipment to one institution in the world, similar to the UN. In that case, we do not require every country to acquire defense equipment and compete with other countries. Every country coming together would create one military power for the entire world, saving trillions of dollars. We could very well spend these astonishing amounts for the well-being of humanity and promote the basic needs of food, shelter, education, and jobs. It would empower society to travel and experience nature without any boundaries. This would help unite humanity and glorify life and creation by experiencing the incredible creation and seeing marvelous places and their phenomena, unfolding breath-taking moments.

**Navya**: Great ideas; one would call them a utopian world?

**Dhaval**: Certainly, we can try to promote a utopian world if that is required for living in freedom to celebrate life. Then politics, economics, education, religion, and customs would be ideal, more or less perfect, and people would try to improve because of the ideal environment. The world would become one big continent without physical borders. Everyone would become a global citizen, enjoying peace and prosperity, freely traveling, working, and residing in different parts of the world without visas!

**Bala**: Would capitalism allow the world to become a utopia?

**Dhaval**: Capitalism is not all-evil. Capitalism has helped spur multiple examples of human ingenuity and invention. But we must now ask ourselves: Isn't it time to move on? Capitalism has got us to where we are now, and it's time for a new form of policies, systems, and government to be the way forward. This would help us restore balance in this global village we all now find ourselves members of, whether we like it or not.

**Manal**: Certainly, we require transformation and new ways to provide opportunities for all in the world.

**Dhaval**: Now it is the time to question if it's right anymore for the world to have two sets of citizens, one percent of the global citizens who can hold 50% of the world's wealth and another 800 million going hungry to bed every night. We need to wake up now to provide everyone with food and education, and only these two necessities can spring this world into real progress to celebrate life for all, living in peace and prosperity.

**Bala**: Surely there is enough in this world for everyone to live happily but not enough for every man's greed! Only this truth can set this world free forever!

**Dhaval**: The entire creation suffers when we hold on to the wealth beyond our requirements, but when we share and care with what we have, we and the world as a whole would be given back in full measure.

**Manal**: That would be love conquering all and everything in this world. The creation is bound by love and processes. By love and laws of processes, we could bring abundant life to this creation to live in bliss and richness. We could learn from the past and look for the great future, but we must act in the present without holding on or attaching to what we don't need. This would promote opportunity, equality, generosity, justice, righteousness, and bliss. Therefore, we must act now through love, caring, and sharing in the present for a beautiful future to fulfill the creator's glory.

**Navya**: We could still make amendments to everything and give out freely what we have in excess. Everyone has something in excess and everything they require when that excess is shared.

**Dhaval**: Certainly, Navya, when we accept our mistakes, the universe will make us walk again in our purpose, and the truth will set us free not far from today!

# CHAPTER 59 ISOLATION

Now I have fame, philosophy, a doctorate, and several publications and dialogues. Everyone looked at me as their guru, all came to me for solutions to their problem, and I gave them advice for all of their problems. People put me on a pedestal, followed my words, my style, and everything I did, and thought I was a messiah to resolve all their problems. I had become a hero for many people and many societies. All wanted a glimpse of me like a movie star, many wanted me to be an adviser, board member, or mentor, and my university wanted me to be a vice-chancellor. People waited hours to meet me; millions followed me endlessly on social media, and the numbers increased by millions daily. One would have thought I had fulfilled everything, wisdom and wealth, became a tall personality, and there would be nothing more to do, achieve, or dream about.

Yet my life and fate hung in the balance. I felt empty within myself, and I was isolated within myself. I thought the knowledge, degrees, status, wealth, personality, power, fame, spirituality, and people putting me on the pedestal would give me enlightenment. But I felt there was no real enlightenment, or I lacked real enlightenment, knowledge, and wisdom that would bring true joy within oneself in all life situations. Though physically I had achieved everything and people were proud of my achievements and success, I was still searching for the reality of life, what life is all about, what true enlightenment means, and what celebrating life every day in every situation means. I didn't have answers to any questions or solutions to my problems!

So, all those people who have achieved so much, the movie starts, sports personalities, scientists, philosophers, businesspeople, political and economic leaders, writers, artists, singers, and professionals, are they not joyful at all times in their life? Why do some of the prominent, mighty, powerful, talented, notable artists and stars become depressed and sometimes end their own lives? What is life all about, then? Life is not about fame, power, wealth, millions of natural and social media followers, respect, personality, and positions?

These things haunted me daily, though I went out to meet my commitments of meeting people, chairing meetings, giving seminars, making big statements, telling people what to do and what not to do, and coaching youth on success. I was only physically present in those events and meetings as my mind, heart, and soul refused to accompany me. Finally, my body became tired, and there was no more inspiration to go about and no more conviction in my talks, advice, and coaching. Soon, a day came when I started to withdraw from these events and seminars, and my physical life came to a grinding halt.

Did that make a difference? Perhaps it did make a difference to some people looking up to me to change some of the chronic issues the society and the people were facing. Some were happy that I was no more visible than I used to be, especially the powerful and ruling elite, for their power and position were threatened, at least to some degree. Some people trolled me, saying I didn't walk the talk, and others made fun of me, judged me, or questioned me about what I was trying to do. Some thought I was taking a break from my schedule and going away on some tour, sightseeing, or relaxing like elites or movie and business stars.

Opinions and judgments didn't matter much as I was still trying to find what life was all about, and I was sure it was not about pleasing people out there or doing what people wanted me to do. There was no point in hanging around though I had achieved everything, yet life was empty and isolated. Ultimately after a few quiet days, I decided to go away from all that limelight, from the university, from the buzz of the world, the noise of the people, and media glare, into nature, an ocean shore close to Paradise. For fear of people noticing me, I traveled at night with a backpack on a bus, the same route as the Western Ghats, bringing back the memories of memories though I couldn't see much visually. Life had come a full three-hundred-and-sixty-degree circle searching for something, though I felt steps were significantly closer this time.

I stayed at a guest house on the beach, watching the shore, its beautiful dancing waves, and the people going about their daily visit to the temple through my window. I ate a little and walked on the beach, marking my legs on the sand. I walked to the temple and back many times for seven days. This brought back the alignment of the soul, mind, and heart to the body. This time there was no tiredness, no more anxiety, but there was hope. I hoped to find out what life is all about sooner than later.

How did all that turn around so quickly? Perhaps connecting back to nature made all the difference. It reminded me of my philosophy of the importance of connecting to the creator; no matter what it is, any product, plant, or living being has to have a connection with the creator. Nothing can exist in this world by itself, all existence has a cause beyond oneself, and anything that wouldn't connect to the creator wouldn't sustain for a long time. And everything in this world has a purpose; nothing has been created or will be made without purpose. Sometimes we may require changing the highway we travel to fulfill our purpose. Only by connecting to the creator can anyone fulfill its purpose and ultimate life cycle, like cars are serviced every five thousand or ten thousand kilometers until they are disposed of.

Similarly, anything broken can only be repaired or corrected, or guided by the creator or someone trained by the creator. Mercedes has to be fixed by itself; Toyota can't repair Mercedes. Like mobile phones, cars, and many other things, we also need to connect to the creator to continue to rejuvenate life and fulfill our purpose.

Haven't I found my purpose yet? Perhaps not! It sometimes unfolds so slowly that we need to wait with patience. Every step in that direction would make us know our purpose sooner than later. But one thing is certain, life without purpose is misery. This had already been experienced, and now I looked for the ultimate purpose of my life. On the seventh day, as I circled the beach and the temple, my sight fell on a tall, brightly dressed person. I went closer, and we faced head-on after so many years. We were no more strangers and recognized each other more so by our voices.

"Dave, come home. Your father he's very ill. I am on the way to see him after many years; a few days back, I got the news that he is critical. Before reaching Paradise, I came here to pray for him and you that you would see your dad and showcase what you have achieved. Almighty planned to meet you here," Aunt Vidya hugged me, caressed me, and held me in her arms for five minutes. In that deep, silent hug, all our emotions and feelings transferred between each other without uttering words like data transfer from one device to another through Bluetooth, and we came to know each other's lives and situations.

"How tall and how handsome you have become, Dave! You were always in my prayers, and all those prayers, wishes, and your mother's blessings have brought you where you are today. I prayed and meditated daily for you at my Ashram in Rishikesh on the Ganges. I always knew that you are destined for something big, no matter what you went through at your dad's hand and perhaps afterward. I have watched your dialogues and breathtaking philosophy and still think that the pinnacle of your life is yet to come, and you will change the world when that happens."

And our faces, hearts, mind, and soul connected to understand all that happened in those years.

# CHAPTER 60 REUNION

Strobing light shone before my eyes. I ran to the guest house, packed my backpack, and checked out in one go by the time Aunt Vidya came to pick me up in her hired taxi. The slides in my mind's projector were dimmed now, more faded; it all felt too surreal. The city roads were bustling, and while the lanes were supposed to have only one vehicle per lane, it was possible to fit in twice or thrice as many, including two and three-wheelers. That's the way it works in India.

In that slow movement, Aunt Vidya had gone into a deep slumber as she had traveled for two days from Rishikesh to Mangalore. Perhaps she was at peace with herself that she found me and connected to the power beyond in gratitude, even in her sleep. When I looked over, her face had a smile with closed eyes, giving me so much serenity that she, too, had played a great role in where I am today, being there for me at Paradise and through her ashram life and meditation.

I had nothing to do other than look out of the window. The landscape was forever changing, and the bright afternoon sun lit up the surrounding countryside. Every few kilometers, I encountered another stunning view, another jungle or small town or village where people were going about their lives. And I was reminded of another world I once lived in, a world I once called home.

Towns turned into villages and villages into towns and towns into cities and cities into fields and fields into mountains. The mountains on either side of me were light golden in the bright sunshine, and the peaks glistened.

Buses full of passengers traveling along the road, many were hanging from the door rails. Others hung hammocks from the luggage rails and slept in those like babies being rocked side to side by the constant motion of the train. All the windows were open for the calm wind to blow. Through the windows, the beaming sun cast its way through the crowd of passengers, chasing out the darkness.

I looked through the window and saw trees and waterlogged fields streaming by as if my waking life was an absolute dream. I watched flashes of scenery and roadside shanty towns that punctuated the journey. Views of deep valleys and terraced hillsides, often following streams and rivers flowing into the sacred Netravati, streets turning into roads and roads turning to little more than dirt tracks.

I pressed my face against the lowered glass window and felt the cold glass against my skin. In time, I fell asleep to the constant burr of the vehicle's engine. I was on the edge of the seat to put a hand on to balance myself, for the road was full of potholes, and along the way, the edges of the road had slid into mud torrents, too, so the driver could never choose a straight line to drive. I thought that was very much the story of my life as I had never traveled in a straight line.

Outside, I saw a small market set up on the trackside. The car had slowed down as we were passing through a small village. From afar, I could see the train passing through. The villagers were congregating and loading up the stalls with all sorts of goods; fruit and vegetables, trinkets, hardware, clothes, flowers, chickens, and ducks. There was a beautiful old temple, contrasting with the street of rundown concrete slabs. In the village square, young women made cakes and pastries with their bare hands. You see, in the village, everyone, men and women, young and old, is connected to the land, or so it seems.

# CHAPTER 61 LIFE'S FULL CIRCLE

Arriving back at the mansion in Mangalore, I had only my small backpack of meager belongings, much as I had left. My heart pounded with memories and pain at the same time as the taxi passed through the colonial entrance gate and old driveway. When I reached the house in the shade of an areca nut tree, I saw that the house structure was much the same as the way I had left it, but the estate had changed substantially. It was no longer the lush rainforest but now had fallen in parts to ruin. The land looked worn as if an abusive lover had mistreated it over the years. The house looked shabby, with bits of the front facade crumbling, the paint of the colonial windows scabbing, the garden footpath to the house disorganized, and weeds growing in the front yard.

Before I could keep my backpack down and make sense of what was happening, a doctor visited the residence. She updated me on my father's current condition. "It's cancer, Mr. Sonsoil. He is fighting hard, but I do not know if he will make it. He has been very sick, and he will not leave his bed. But he was asking for you, Mr. Sonsoil, and I want you to listen carefully. We are trying our best to put this tumor into remission, but..."

"Then he must be sent to the hospital."

"He has very little time," replied the doctor solemnly. "He is not here to get better, Dhaval; he is here to die."

I pushed open the door to see my father asleep. Aunt Vidya was already there, praying and interceding for my dad, providing a lot of brightness in the room. It was just getting dark. The orange hues of sunset flooded through the windows, marking their crisscrossed patterns against the white walls and lighting the room golden green, brown, and red. Many machines blinked off and on. The sound of rain was now so very dim against the bedroom windows. Around his bed sat many cards and heart-shaped balloons with pretty ribbons that his friends and business partners had sent him. He did not wake. Not knowing what to do with myself, I pulled up a chair toward his bedside, sat down, and looked over him as Aunt Vidya left the room for her evening meditation.

He looked up at me. I had not realized how much grey was streaking his hair.

"Dad, I am sorry, I could not hold on. I am so sorry."

He was weak, but his voice was firm. He didn't know if he would make it, but he could not bear to let go. "I would want you to live your life and be happy. You are the apple of my eye, my child, and you must not cry."

I felt his warm body limp, and I thought he was dying. In a panic, I screamed, "No, no, no!"

He did not respond. It seemed he was passing on, but he was not. My father opened his eyes and smiled at me. "They are trying their best to put this tumor into remission, but..."

"Tell me your story," dad said, turning his pale yellow eyes.

"Dad, I am very close to finding what life is all about. It is all about celebrating but without holding on to anything, sharing and caring, going through the loss, grief, difficulties, suffering, and hardships, and at the same time, encountering new ways, new thinking, new inventions, new sights, new music, new drama, new cinema, new language, new place and so on. When not attached to this world, life unravels itself with utmost love and truth, celebrating every moment, filling heart, mind, soul, and being in the joy of glorifying the creation."

He coughed a little, and his lungs' dark shadows protruded under the sheets. "But..." he struggled, "Everything must have its time, and everything is temporary. If only I had known that earlier in my life. It took me my whole life to realize the important things, Dhaval. And the most important thing to me was always you."

My father was frail, and I felt that strange heavy feeling in my chest when I saw my mother passed away. I watched as he slept and soon fell into a deep slumber. When he finally stirred and opened his eyes, I let him know of my love for him by telling him I always loved him.

"Dave? Dave? Dave? You still love me?" He asked. I saw him slowly opening his eyes and trying to focus on me.

I replied sleepily, just like him, "Yes, father. Dave still loves you."

"It's been so many years ..." Father said. "Did you make something of yourself?"

"I did, Father. I traveled around India and became a philosopher, writer, and life coach, proclaiming coming-of-age philosophy to the world."

That night, my father passed away in his sleep.

# CHAPTER 62 THE SOUL

My father was buried with my mother, as he had wanted. There was no rock music this time, and it was more your somber, usual, expected funeral. As a hermit, Aunt Vidya took the lead and chanted all the mantras. They provided much-needed serenity, tranquility, and repose to dad's soul. Some of the relatives and many of dad's friends attended the funeral and were happy to see me at the funeral. Many hugged me, whispering about what dad had done for them.

After the funeral, some relatives and friends came home, lit a big candle, and placed it below the massive portrait of dad that hung on the center wall of the living room. The mourning lasted for four days, with daily chanting of mantras, preparing dad's favorite meals, and placing a plate in front of dad's photo. In the evening, the dish was taken out to feed the birds of Paradise. On the fourth day, all the relatives and dad's friends were invited for a day-long mourning, eulogy, meals, rituals, and chanting of mantras led by Aunt Vidya. Many local temple priests joined, remembering dad's contribution to their temple. I was happy to see so many people, especially relatives. They were glad to see Aunt Vidya, and they all respected her new-found, commanding, spiritual personality. Finally, the time came to bid farewell to Aunt Vidya as she left, perhaps for the final time, Paradise to Rishikesh. I wanted her to stay back, but she wanted to continue her hermit life, where she found everything she wanted, even her life purpose. I thought so because she was full of life, always smiling, calm, no questions asked, and so on. She hugged me long enough, whispering in my ears what she had told me years before, "Dave, you are to change the world sooner than later, and you are right on the track. My prayers will continue for you and your mission."

I learned that my father had left me everything in his will. The entire Mangalore estate, the old home in Bangalore, and several other properties and shares of many business enterprises in Bangalore and around the country. What will I do with such a vast amount of wealth? One thing I knew was that I couldn't bury them without using them; if I deposited the wealth without good use, that would soon disappear. I stood on the balcony, and my senses came back to me. From that vantage, I could see more clearly into the distance. The leaves of the oak trees shone like patches of wet, blue velvet, static now forever like dust upon their branches. The glow of the city still seeped into the sky permanently. The waves no longer reached the shore but glowed, unmoved like the white veins of dark-blue marble.

Now I wandered much like a ghost in the mansion. In some places, the vines had crept through the windows; in other areas, the mildew had seeped along the walls, but there were remnants here, and there of a life I once lived, a dash of joy and beauty, a life of wonder, before that warmth in my heart had retreated in my mother's death and the floods and the storm of life. Sometimes I would pause and hold my breath for a moment and imagine myself running through the vast halls, the sea of black velvet and light blue mahogany surrounding me, to see a more delicate, warmer golden glow.

I sat by the door. On the sill, I could see the image of a boy looking out over the landscape. I felt a kind of emptiness around me. A loneliness that I had not known for a long time. And in that loneliness, I felt there was no meaning to existence. Or perhaps, it was the absence of purpose, a death that brought about a heaviness of heart, an indescribable weight, a sense of crushing under a boulder that I hadn't known before.

Time went by, as they all do. Every day, everything seemed the same. It was only when I would get up late in the evening without doing my morning exercises, and go to sleep without watching the sunrise, every day, every night, every moment, that I would feel as if it was all slipping away from me. Then I would get angry with myself for not being free from all that darkness, not being able to shed it like fur and see the light again.

I became aware I was shaking all over. That odd feeling returned, pulling me like I was no longer attached to the ground, like I was about to fly off into the stratosphere on an elastic band. I was sure I was levitating for a moment, but I looked down at my feet to see I was still very much on the ground.

Finally, it hit me. I had never before felt such emptiness. An emptiness that burned like hunger, leaving me numb. It was as if that giant glowing light I had seen in my youth had faded and no longer was there as a spark of joy in my heart. There was only sorrow. What the Portuguese call saudade, the Welsh call hiraeth, the Romanians call dor, and the Ethiopians call Zita. Grief for the lost or departed. I was suffering for the love that remains. The grief I felt in the core of what the Russians call dusha—the soul.

It's difficult to explain exactly what went through my mind as I once again remembered my parents' death. A mixture of fear and sadness would be an understatement, and it was so exact that it could not be completely put into words. A feeling, not of loss, regret, or something missing, but something inextricably and miraculously slipping away into the nothingness that I felt in the core of my entire being. I felt it in my stomach, surging through every pore and every bone of my whole body—a feeling of profound, universal energy that can usually only be found in the plasma of stars.

However, fast time had moved to that point in my life; it stopped there, and then like a polaroid, life froze in time. I remember everything about that moment. Everything. I remember that surge of pure adrenaline through my veins. But the subtle things too. The scent of the linoleum floor, the lavender scent of the freshly laundered linen.

# CHAPTER 63 MEMORY

I could never understand this world of misery, and I still dreamt of it. There were times when I was awake, and I would see the light as a prism on the walls, or the branches of the trees, as the sun shone behind them, as rain fell in a light mist upon them, as though I had created my world, my bubble of peace in the universe. But then, at other times, it is just as it was; dark, just as the rains fell, just as the clouds rolled through, just as a smile filled my lips and I could taste a sour wine. Just as when I try to recollect some long-forgotten memory, the things I have tried so hard to forget, the things I have been attempting to push aside, I could remember the little details of the face of the woman who was the first love of my life when I held her in my arms and kissed her.

The rain in the evening is like love—a soft kiss. The first rays of light falling on the walls in the morning are like a ray of love—a kiss on the forehead. Greeting a stranger, like a lover with a smile, and you have shared a kiss. A smile, an embrace, a kiss, and you have shared a cup of tea.

I think those are the things that made me happy. When I was awake, when I was conscious, when I was awake to myself, I felt the soul and love. This world was just a memory of myself—another kind of memory, perhaps, but a memory nonetheless. I felt now in the nothingness that I gave meaning to my life. And I gave meaning to the little things. Everything to me was sacred in the world. Everything was precious. Returning to the courtyard, I emerged into the bright sunlight and felt a sudden humming in my ear of another frequency. I suddenly felt frozen not by time but by fear, for something else that I could not see had suddenly, like a faint mist, run through my body and out through the other side. The hairs on my neck stood on end.

As I searched for the kitchen, I wandered into a bedroom. Where does a person hide their secrets? I wondered as I opened a cupboard. My eyes were instantly drawn to a dust-covered cardboard shoe box on the bottom shelf, and I pulled it out onto the carpet floor. Inside I found an envelope, inside of which was a birthday card with the message, "Happy Birthday, Dhaval." Underneath this was a photo of me with a pre-university certificate in my hands, and I was beaming a smile. I realized father must have kept it.

Returning to reality, I stepped into the kitchen. Dishes were again piled high in the kitchen sink. The place stank. It was like the scene of some train wreck that had occurred the night before. A train had crashed right into the building. It was the train of depression, tragedy, loneliness, unhinged, a whole list of things I had been carrying with me all through my life. And now it was as if that train had flattened me, had finally caught up with me, and brought the total tonnage of disaster upon me.

I slept that night in my old room. In the morning, the sharp sun rays stung my eyes from the window, waking me up. Each day I listened again to the sounds of the birds flying over the Paradise rainforest and countryside, the sounds of the rustling leaves, that same symphony of nature and of my youth I hadn't heard for so many years. Again, I was living a life of isolation. The life of the loner was a life I had grown accustomed to. For most of my life, that's all I had ever known.

I spent the next seven days mostly sitting in the garden, not knowing the next step in my life. All I knew was that I felt empty again. And now my mind was filled with a new photograph, the image of the last sight of my father.

Looking into the distance, I saw the storm clouds rolling up and over the mountains, like a tsunami in the sky, heading for me. It threatened to black out the sun completely. I didn't know how long it would be before it caught up with me.

I could once again see all of Paradise stretched out before me. I remembered my mother, her gardening, and the flowers. I still remember how the petals seemed to sway in a magical breeze of their world across my vision on that day she had shown me the dandelion. And as if she were there in front of me, I felt I could smell that same floral scent again.

Like the Jagganath vehicles, I realized they were like time, forever rolling forwards. Everyone wants to be on the cars in the parade, but no one can get on them, everyone follows behind, and some get caught under the juggernaut, trampled by time.

What had become of me and my life? Standing in the hallway, I felt sudden vertigo. Black, red, and purple shapes rolled over my vision like drunken amoebas though I was sure I had not closed my eyes this time. But it was memories of the years and in the morning, looking out over the sunrise over the field's newness that hit me.

Love and gratitude are the two most precious things that keep life going regardless of the situation. Gratitude for surviving those situations provides new hope and direction, and I was content with that. I felt I had found an answer, at least in some form. There was still no blowout, but I started to question whether that was ever possible, that it was just something that had spread like Chinese whispers, but really, the blowout was just a simple realization to let go.

Perhaps it was the storm and mother nature's redemption; maybe it was seeing the landscape broken, things change, and life diverting like that river, but whatever the reason. I saw my life suddenly snaking out in multiple directions, tentacles of fate, all possibilities leading to new horizons, to a brand-new sea. And I realized I was now a completely different person, and the realization ran full circle that I was not only a new person but also a transience, as all things are transient.

I understood then what the guru in the ashram had told me. Power is not the juggernaut. Power is surrender. For there is an old Indian proverb: if you conquer your mind, you will conquer the world. And your mind is the world. They are one. The very idea that you are one thing separate from anything else is a false assumption. There is no such thing as one thing. Never was. Everything was always two; we were all linked.

How can you go through your life without breaking anything? Without getting hurt? Life is a juggernaut. Life cannot stop. The sprout and the screw. The sage and the fool. You cannot escape it. Rich and poor alike, you cannot escape it. But power is not in the juggernaut. No. Power is in the person who understands that life will not stop, knowing they will be broken, that they will be torn, that they will fail, that they will succeed, that they will laugh, that they will cry, that they will shout, that they will scream. Power is the person who walks through the hail of bullets with no promise of love, fame, or redemption, but in search of silence, calm, beauty, and good. Power is the person who gets knocked down and gets up again to face their destruction. Power is surrender, and surrender is freedom.

Then I realized that the power of surrender only could be realized and experienced when we go beyond ourselves, loving beyond one's self, caring, respecting, and loving everything and everyone around us, and living in gratitude and communion with all and everything around us. My heart and mind came together to end my self-induced isolation and go out and meet people and nature to experience the power of surrender and freedom. I made all the plans to be out there from tomorrow, surrendering all my ego, status, education, degrees, philosophy, me and I, to live in communion with everyone and everything around me.

# CHAPTER 64 PANDEMIC

That evening all my plans came crashing down as my social media handles beeped on my phone, "Lockdown, Lockdown, protect yourself and loved ones by social distancing." Curiously I switched on the TV, and the only news every channel gave was that the government had ordered locking down the entire country from midnight to arrest the spread of a deadly virus, delivering 1.3 billion people only four hours' notice. Every village, district, town, and state was ordered to lock down for weeks without even providing details of how and when one could get their essential items from the market to survive. Though I was already in self-declared isolation, not allowing going out and being with nature and people around me as planned was like losing my freedom from this day onwards. Yet I thought I would find a way once the morning sun gave way to the darkness of the night.

When I woke up in the morning, my phone was continuously flooded with surreal images and videos on social media handles. The poor men and women migrant workers, carrying their bags and children on their heads and in arms, were walking in the darkness of the night on the highways towards their remote destinations. Journalists' interaction with these India's poorest showed that they feared they would starve and have to sleep on the streets, and they started their exodus by queuing up in millions at various railway stations at midnight. And when they heard that their only affordable means of public transport, such as trains and buses, were also locked down, they started walking kilometers, losing hope of any help from authorities.

My heart melted, I empathized with them, and my mind got into a tangle to do something for them. After a quick morning wash and breakfast, I hurried and walked straight to the Paradise workers' leaders on the river banks. This was my first visit to their colonies after my return, and though they were happy to see me, they were not forthcoming, perhaps of the fear that I was like my dad, who ruled over them with an iron fist. But I sat with them on the floor, asking them if they knew about the lockdown and if they had enough essentials to survive a few days until we came to know the arrangements from the authorities for the essential items to be purchased. Mingling with the so called untouchables gave them the courage to open up, perhaps for the first time, though still in some fear. News spread around the colony in no time, and all the elders and women surrounded me.

One after, other older men enquired about me and my well-being, and slowly people took the courage to speak to me, offering me condolences and emphasizing the loss of my dad. Then women followed them, and they provided me an Arathi with lights and flowers, a Hindu tradition of welcoming a guest or owner or a returned loved one. I was mesmerized by their honor, respect, and love. Now all the youth and children joined the elders to catch a glimpse of me like I was some celebrity. But I stood up and went towards them, greeting every one of them. I could hear their murmurs, "He is not like his dad, he is different, and he wants to meet us, speak to us." Others said, "Let's tell him our struggles, unpaid wages, dilapidated huts, and our children's struggles."

Now the elders started telling me their stories, one after the other, of all those years I wasn't in Paradise. Tears rolled down their cheeks, and my eyes swelled with tears. All my emotions broke loose, and my heart broke for the second time. Silence ruled for some time as if all were empathizing with each other, and in that silence, several thoughts came to my mind, "Why do mortals accumulate without giving what was due to others or giving at least some part of their hard-earned wealth for those who made it possible? Why don't we allow others to become prosperous? Why don't we share, care and love people around us and provide them with their basic needs?"

Now the silence was broken by a youth who reminded me that it was a lockdown and we were not supposed to meet. But elders responded that there was no virus in Paradise and the virus can't dare to enter Paradise, bringing us much laughter after all those high emotions and tears. "Today, you would have everything, and we will work together to better our Paradise and our state, country, and the world," I assured them to much cheer of all assembled. I asked the leaders to provide details of every family's unpaid wages and needs and asked the youths to follow me to the warehouse complex of the estate. To my surprise, I could see that the number of warehouses had doubled since I had left, and all were filled with variety of rice, wheat, and grains. Two contrasting images flashed in my mind; one was that people were going hungry and walking kilometers for food and safety; the other was that people were hoarding and accumulating, yet unable to use or utilize their wealth in their lifetime.

I made two groups of youth, giving responsibility to one group to distribute the grains to all the needy families in Paradise and asked the other group to follow me using the vehicles of Paradise to the nearby highways to look for the migrants. And it seemed that the pandemic aided in surrendering my power to bring freedom to me and the people around me.

# CHAPTER 65 EUREKA

During the pandemic, there was no room for the poor, and they were left to find their way to survival and protection against the virus. It was challenging for the millions of migrant Indian workers to reach their remote villages thousands of kilometers away. Without any work or compensation and exhausted resources, men and women tried to escape from hunger and homelessness in the cities and urban centers with children in their arms, balancing their belongings on their heads. They were walking day and night on highways in the soaring temperatures of 40 degrees while some traveled by bicycle or any other transport that was barely available.

The sweat dripped from their head like a drizzle soaking their clothes as their feet's friction with the asphalt bruised, cut, and scabbed their soles and fingers, while the sharp sunrays cracked their skin. Some fell from exhaustion without the energy to walk any further; some fainted with swollen feet, others were nauseous, and others were running out of food and water. They were all tired, and their body was aching; some had a fever, while many could hardly breathe, and their eyes were full of tears. There were no protection masks, medicine, or clinics on the highways. Their only protection against the virus was their long shawls covering their mouth. Their visuals of helplessness on TV and social media punctured holes in many people's hearts, including mine.

As we reached the highway, the sight of helplessness in front of our eyes shivered me and the youth of Paradise. This reminded me of the horror stories my aunt told me about India's partition in 1947, where millions of people walked kilometers to cross the border from either side and how over a million people couldn't see the next day. We swung into action, offering migrant laborers to sit in our vehicles to take a deep breath by sipping water and lemonade. Then we provided them shelter, food, and a play area for children at Paradise, and most of them took this offer, bringing a smile back to their faces. Hundreds of people were ferried every hour into Paradise and provided packs of food and water for those very few who wanted to carry on.

A new chapter began at Paradise, albeit roles were reversed for the first time. So far, people worked for Paradise; now, Paradise started working for the people. The Paradise community came together, emptying the warehouses to shelter thousands of people. Women cooked food; others sewed linen face masks, and children played with migrant children giving them hope. People took turns working round the clock, youth driving the entire operation, patrolling highways day and night, and transporting thousands of people daily to Paradise. They delivered food to the vulnerable and needy in and around the city. While returning, they brought essential items such as mattresses, pillows, free-size dresses, towels, etc.

In a few days, Paradise became a vast center for migrant, needy and vulnerable people. People came from all directions of the city to help build showers, toilets, isolation centers, mega kitchens, etc. With people crisscrossing all around, the virus also found its entry. Paradise and the city community ran against the time, building a field hospital and hi-tech laboratory in no time. Engineers, erectors, workers, doctors and nurses, para medicals, and nursing students came in huge numbers caring for and looking after thousands of people.

Yet there was no panic, though infected cases surged. Everyone was calm and followed safety protocols by wearing masks and maintaining good hygiene. Everyone did their work, everything fell in place, and nothing was lacking. Food, materials, medicines, doctors, and nurses were available around the clock. News spread thick and fast, and people from all walks of life who were infected took shelter in Paradise. The field hospital expanded multifold to cater to the influx of people from surrounding cities, districts, and villages. Everyone helped each other; everyone knew their role, did what they were supposed to do, and accepted to serve the people they were assigned to. Leaders led well, respecting all as equals, and the moment they found leadership in others, they willingly relinquished their roles and became servants. All took the decision together, actively listening to everyone and sharing their ideas, values, and dreams.

All people who came to serve shared what they had in excess, food grains, money, time, knowledge, expertise, and encouragement. Grains, vegetables from vast areas of all types of vegetable cultivation, and the amount of money in bank accounts never ran out. Nature and people worked together for all the needy, sick, and vulnerable. All cared with the healing touch, kindness, empathy, respect, and generosity that overflowed to arrest the pandemic in and around Paradise. This comforted people in their struggles. It was truly remarkable that not a single life was lost in nature's paradise by serving people and becoming a servant of everyone through servant leadership.

I wondered how all this happened, what made people come together, what made them share selflessly what they had in excess, listen to everyone and share their ideas and expertise. How did leaders take on all opinions, ideas, and views and discerned the best for all? Why no one held on to the power and authority? Why everyone respected each other without judging their status, caste, and creed?

Swiftly I realized that I knew what was happening and about to happen like the young Buddha. Whether it was the heaviness of the wind or some sensation of higher gravity, I guess it was all of the above, but abruptly I felt transported and somehow connected to something bigger than myself. I somehow knew that this was a milestone. All came together because they transformed and attached their heart to nature, the creator, and when they connected to the creator, they had all known their life purpose, the purpose for that moment, and the resources for this gigantic mission. Everyone associated with this mission knew their unique task and performed their work to perfection, giving victory to them and everyone in Paradise. Suddenly I was struck with a eureka moment like Archimedes, and the big cry within me gushed out, "Eureka, Eureka, Eureka!"

Life is about connecting to nature, the people around us, and the creator; to live, experience, and celebrate every moment in every situation.

At that moment, the eureka light flashed continuously within me and reminded my philosophical dialogues, "Nothing exists in this world by itself, and everything that exists has to connect with the creator for an optimal life cycle, like a mobile phone connecting to the creator to update and download the software and apps now and then." If it doesn't update the software and apps, it may not perform to its potential and ultimately withers away. And not only do all that connect to the creator celebrate its optimal life cycle, but those who are using its services and the creator both celebrate and glorify the creation. Our life, too, will wither away like a broken chair or mirror losing its purpose if we do not connect to the creator.

Why eureka now? Because I was in communion with the people and nature and started celebrating life by sharing and caring, perhaps coming to know my mission, which I had not known until then. So far, I tried to find and live life, and when we do that, we get lost in attempting to acquire all kinds of things, love, knowledge, status, positions, wealth, and power. The world is made for humans and not humans for the world. The world should follow us to celebrate every moment of our lives and glorify creation. When we celebrate life, all we require automatically follows us, knowledge, love, wealth, status, and power. We would never be inclined to attach to these temporary things as we celebrate daily life. If we follow the world, we will get lost in trying to acquire all that world offers and will never shake off those attachments to celebrate life.

# CHAPTER 66 REVISITOR

Journalists and TV channels helped to spread the news of the eureka phenomenon beyond the boundaries of Paradise. Many people and visitors thronged Paradise in protective gear to experience the magnitude of people sharing and caring without any significant fear during the pandemic when million were dying worldwide. News anchors and presenters interviewed people from all walks of life. They dwelled deep into how Paradise became the shelter for migrants and communities, how everyone suddenly became so generous, caring, and sharing, and how everyone got united without judging anyone for their religion and caste.

Now was the time for me to step back as talented and inspiring people started leading from the front. After many days spent with the Paradise family and people, guiding, arranging resources, caring, eating, and sleeping in the community, I intended to return home to the mansion when something stopped me. I watched the intriguing Indian roller with its colorful combinations of feathers and spellbinding Persian blue tail flying high, descending in a circular motion, rapidly flapping its wings. I followed it. It was a beautiful day, and though it was late afternoon, I decided I didn't want to go home and linger in the place of my memories. I wanted to be free of all that.

So, I followed the bird, and it took me to the jungle in a drizzling rain over the landscape of Mangalore. It was humid but cool, and I smelt the familiar scents from my childhood of lime and incense in the air from somewhere afar. I have always loved those scents, and there were times when I was away from Paradise, but those scents still seemed to drift to me from afar. I found myself walking toward the love-heart tree, bringing back all those memories. It was the saddest scene. From afar, I could see the strong tree stood out like a sore thumb in the jungle. The oak leaves had begun to turn an ugly brown. That's why I had stopped here for a moment. As I stood there, I could see the shadows of two people carrying flowers and walking off, like the shadows from something that had died. Or perhaps like my memory of my parents, their hands clinging onto one another as they sat drifting off to sleep in their armchairs in the lounge, sad but inevitable. I tried to let go of the tears flowing down my cheeks, thinking it was not much to cry over. It would not be the last time I would feel this way. I stepped back for a moment, almost dizzy, feeling that I was wrong, that it had all been an illusion from the start.

I turned back and instantly felt the presence of someone behind the tree. This was fate meeting me face to face.

I felt a whirring in my stomach again, like a washing machine, and it went quiet when it reached such a speed. I walked straight to the love-heart tree. When I got there, I saw the clearing was empty. I looked over the fields and saw the yellowing light bathing the fields and the trees. Around the tree hung a bright yellow silk ribbon, and I stopped as a sudden thought hit me. A gentle hum hit the air.

I saw Asha in between the barks of the two trees. I watched her for a moment, her face, her eyes, her smile, that familiar warmth that had once covered her like a child, wrapped up in an old blanket soaked in the scent of the forest. I bent my head to see Asha and ensure I was no longer dreaming. Then she, too, stepped forward, and we both moved toward each other slowly. We stopped at arm's length distance. I raised my hand to her face as the tears streamed down her cheek.

Adrenaline surged. My body came alive like an electric fire. The veins in my temples twitched. Before I could even think about what I was doing, some automatic, perhaps even primordial, quadrant of my brain had decided to act, and I was walking toward her.

The world seemed to spin again, and the living room dissolved once more, and new things were forged in the darkness, rock rose through the mist, and that blue thread again spun around her. In a valley covered by a sea of yellow chrysanthemums, where golden truffles seemed to glow orange as if they were alive, humming at the base of trees, the sky became a faint maroon and seemed sweet as apple juice. She was there, surrounded by a cloud of dark, light turquoise; the color clouds were painted just heavy with rain and hit by a glow of sunlight. She turned back to me, and we embraced as I drank in that sweet fragrance of her hair and felt the curve of her back.

Her bright, beautiful, yellow dress fluttered in the wind. That wild look in her eyes. I reached out my hand as she reached out her hand.

In my mind, I pictured how everything would play out if my life were a Bollywood film. Suddenly her lips were on mine, my lips were on hers, and my hands were on her hips. She closed her eyes as I edged forwards still and rested back into the air mattress with a sigh, smiling. I breathed in deeply, still soaked with the rain, and her eyes locked on mine. I grabbed her, and we kissed again just as time seemed to play out in slow motion.

I remember that first moment she appeared through the silken leaves of the jungle trees as if through a veil of all I had ever known: her dark brown hair and dark, honey-brown, almond eyes.

Just as Asha placed her head in my hands, turned me to face her, and kissed me, the world was dimmed or put on hold, turned off. I felt an eternity in that kiss; I saw butterflies flutter beneath my eye, bonfires again lit in my bones, and fireworks glittering in my skin. And as the faint light of bonfires faded into the dark of night, the last rays of sunset shone upon the land. There were thick clusters of trees on the outskirts of the upper tier on which the mansion was built. The entire hill was covered with shrubs, and the bloomed little white flowers seemed to glow as they caught the last of the day's light, making the hillside appear speckled as if it were covered in snow. And as the faint light of bonfires started to fade into the dark of night, we made love, and all the many worlds that ever existed in the universe seemed to me then to stop. And everything at the same time suddenly felt in fast motion. In a moment, I thought I saw the glowing orb of light in that storm again, an ominous reminder of something raw, powerful, unknown, and terrifying, the source, the end, the orb of light. But I did.

But my life isn't a Bollywood film.

There was something, too, in the sequin depth of her red-brown eyes and the subtle sadness therein that made me feel as though I were falling into the whirlpool of a supernova. The air was filled with the scent of mangoes and jackfruit, and the sky was tangerine. The kaleidoscope whirled. We breathed each other in. The lightning bolt hit me. Now I knew what it meant to dance upon the skin of another as if their skin was silk. Again, something deep in my soul's bottom fluttered as if nothing had ever beaten. In her eyes, I saw the marvels of the universe, I saw the explosions of supernovas, I saw empires built and turn to dust, I saw the blossoming of all life in slow motion, flowers in perpetual bloom, as we were waves, waves in an infinite ocean, rolling over each other the way young lovers do. In her, I felt the eyes of a universe beheld. In her, I felt the laws of the universe march in procession and stop before me, with me.

And all the time, we stayed together and apart, within each other. We embraced, there in the middle of the night, in the calm between storms, the stars at their farthest point, and she with me, as the darkness swallowed us up in its amorphous form. As we touched and held, I realized I could never separate myself from her again. I could never be alone again. The stars were all there and everywhere. I looked at her face; her eyes were closed, her long black lashes like the light of many galaxies flickering. And as the cold snaked into my bones, the world began to move faster, like a shutter, like the eye of a storm. An eye tried to see the depth of existence, but it was too small to see anything in its heart of it. There was no place I could go where I could be alone and apart from her. We would never be apart again. I felt all creation move slowly in her and the universe be known. In her, I felt the eyes of a universe beheld. And so we ran. We ran. She, with all her might and her laughter in her veins. I with all my hope and with my hopes in her. We were at each other's snot, scenting each other's breath, and in each other's skin forever, not just be with each other. This kind of love never experienced before made me feel content to stay with Asha in every moment of our life; the type of love made us run, laugh, sail, climb and celebrate life. We found what we were looking for, the joy of living, experiencing the depth of love, the true, selfless love, the glue or the catalyst that binds all creation and all people from time immemorial, now and forever.

# CHAPTER 67 CHANGE

Asha, going away from Paradise years ago, had settled in Mumbai with her family with the money that was paid by my father to leave Paradise. There she studied journalism and worked with one of the country's top news channels. She covered the migrants and their woes during the pandemic traveling on highways, and when she heard about the new destination for migrants; she connected immediately with the past and present of Paradise and its community, anchoring some of the best programs for the TV channel.

In some ways, the sudden turnaround and the new direction of growth in Paradise echoed the regrowth of ourselves. All the time, more people joined in caring and sharing, clinging to Paradise's unique way of life. Everywhere I looked, people were caring, loving, sharing, helping, smiling, working in the hospitals, and communities, planting seeds, paddy, shrubs, and trees, and reaping grains, veggies, and fruits.

Gradually, Paradise and the forest became more fertile, and the mansion became more shrouded in green cover. Life started slowing down as Asha, and I cherished every moment together. Slowing down made me pause more, like I did as a child, to feel the sun on my face, the wind in my hair, or the soil in my hands.

The more I integrated myself into the world, my perception shifted. As more and more people came to see the new Paradise and helped the rebuilding effort, they also found a more transparent, more spacious experience. As Paradise and the forest began to heal, the trees started to feel and smell more alive. The moss on the rocks began to glow with a greenish hue. The air was electric with the tang of flowers and trees. The colors were more prosperous and brighter. Paradise and the world around us were speaking in an entirely new voice. It was calling us to live a deeper and more meaningful life; a life never experienced before.

So, with caring and sharing, we brought back Paradise with the help of a new vision. I found that the light shone brighter each time I pushed back the darkness to a smaller size. Every time I released even a tiny percentage of it into the light, the light became brighter. I just had to concentrate on that light, even if it were an ember in the darkness. Moving my will upon it made it grow.

Asha and I planted vegetables and flowers in the vegetable garden, the same garden my mother had tended when I was a young boy. As time went on, we found more joy in being in nature – weeding the garden, watering the plants, and taking photos of the little bugs that landed on the leaves of the vegetables. We planted many more fruit trees, apple trees, pear trees, and tangerines inspired by sunsets, and I told her, "In a few years, these will give us apples, pears, plums, and figs."

It was no Hanging Gardens of Babylon, but we were proud of it. We planted herbs—mint, oregano, thyme, basil, and rosemary—in neat little window boxes. The veggie garden was humble but healthy—spinach, potatoes, and a few onions.

Asha was so happy with the garden that she spent many days there. Even when it was raining, she would sit under an umbrella listening to the water flooding the soil, playing its ancient song as it pelted the small concrete path nestled against the side of the house and surged through the gutters down to the street. She would cozy up in her hammock like a caterpillar in a cocoon, on nights warm enough, by the outside fire that I topped up with firewood. She would lay in the hammock for hours on end, the world blurred to her view, swaying by the wind, feeling the drizzling rain on her face, and listening to the fire crackling.

We planted white flowers all around the house so they would bloom like fresh snow in the spring. Chickens here and there busied themselves kicking up red earth, and all around us, wildlife returned to its rhythm and melody.

We were happy. We were content. We were in the moment.

"For some time now, I can't shake off these premonitions of some unknown doomed fate waiting for us, the feeling that you and I are inevitably destined for a black hole from which there is no escape. To find ourselves at a dead end, as if in a dream, unable to run but eternally being chased. Where is the end? All these last weeks, I wondered how I could always keep you at my side. Without you, there would be no meaning to my life. Remember our conversation about love being a flower that we must not squeeze too tightly? We had that conversation when we were so young and naive, yet we already understood something profound."

There was a long silence.

"I cannot hold you loosely, Dhaval. I cannot. All this time, I've tried to understand who you are," Asha broke the silence.

I smiled. "Letting go is not the same as forgetting. I never told you, but ... I've had dreams in which we were together in different places. I keep thinking; I have this theory, you see, that maybe you and I have lived ten thousand lives together. In each life, like two atoms, we just missed each other and had to roam endlessly around the void of existence for a trillion years to have a chance at bumping into each other again; we just missed grasping our hands in this drifting. Maybe in each life, we just come close to being together and miss out. And then I understood it. You are a dream. You are my dream."

"There is another possibility you left out. What if two lovers existed in two universes?" Asha revealed.

The silvery moonlight glowed through the loose curtain, gently blowing in the open window.

Asha looked at me more sternly. I could see the young girl again in her eyes, disappointed, as if I'd just told her there was no Santa Clause or that she wouldn't be getting a puppy for Christmas. "Dhaval, you mean after all these years, you still have no ending for our love story?"

"That is the ending," I replied. "It was always the ending. Only the first time, I didn't realize it."

"Sometimes endings are not what we expect them to be. But I told you, it was a great story. The story that you never knew where it had started, and you would never know when it ended. When it ended, you wouldn't know how much it affected you till a long time afterward."

"I'm still not so sure that you should be a writer," said Asha jokingly.

"You're probably right," I replied, smiling.

# CHAPTER 68 THE NEW PARADISE

Now the eureka light and wind continuously streamed through Paradise and its occupants, inspiring people to serve and love each other, performing their roles to the best of their ability without judging anyone by their name, caste, religion, and sex. The routine followed every day, people came, people served, people shared, and people from all faiths and walks of life prayed together in their own religion's custom and culture, respecting other beliefs, allowing everyone, embracing the eureka phenomenon in communion with each other, not just to live life but to celebrate life.

The smiling faces and positive strides of everyone at Paradise, even in the middle of the worst pandemic when thousands were dying around the world, every day mesmerized me. There was no fear in anyone; there was no despair, even though many infected people came to Paradise seeking care and relief. No leader panicked, nor any leader said, "We can't handle more people." New volunteers joined Paradise to care for people every day. All hoped they would see better days by celebrating every moment of their life.

It was a romantic paradise. Amid despair, suffering, and fear, all was perfect in Paradise. Nothing was lacking materially, physically, emotionally, or spiritually even when many virus-infected people thronged Paradise. The field hospitals multiplied, and hi-tech laboratories were set up to scientifically screen infected people to understand the resistance and character of the virus, which helped ease the spiraling infections and develop anti-viral treatments and vaccines.

Both rich and poor were given the same treatment, care, honor, and respect; nobody could make a difference in the people's status, caste, or religion. In the new Paradise, the poor became equal to the rich in every aspect, and the rich started sharing their excessive wealth after experiencing the new Paradise. Their joy of sharing didn't leave me and Asha much behind; the numerous properties and equities in many businesses that my father left me went out to meet new owners making Paradise indeed Eden filled with great wealth, care, love, respect, freedom, healing, opportunities and new hope.

How did all this happen? Again eureka light blinked in my mind, "When we live in communion with each other, connecting; we connect with nature and the creator, loving, caring, sharing, and respecting each other, and then we would come to know our purpose and mission, how much wealth and resources we should own, how much should we give, whom and when should we give, seek help when and where we require, understanding every detail to celebrate life."

The Eureka phenomenon started spreading thick and fast beyond everyone's imagination. People from all walks of life came together to give and seek new opportunities in education, health, sports, cinema, business, tourism, spirituality, and so on, building a new paradise, enabling every person to follow their passion and talent, mightily glorifying the creation. The Eureka phenomenon inspired the wealthy, celebrities, sports persons, business people, professionals, musicians, politicians, filmmakers, cinema actors and artists, bureaucrats, writers, poets, young and old, to come together, sharing their talent, passion, excess of wealth and time; setting up their respective fields of specialties with a magnitude of shared wealth, reaching out from the top of the pyramid to the bottom in communion with people, living with the ordinary people, sharing their knowledge, instituting the multitude of independent organizations with all protocols, all systems; for all learning, and skill development, promoting and celebrating the talent using the passion of everyone, without any barriers.

What a joy, what a life, what a new way! At Paradise, everyone knew how much wealth and money they required to live their extraordinary lives, and no one held more than what they needed by sharing their excess. All had everything, excelled in their passion, developing and exhibiting their talent beyond imagination, allowing everyone to shine like a bright star. All knew they were unique, that no one is perfect, and that when others' talent is celebrated, they will develop their aptitude and passion. All sought freedom, truth, sharing, and caring; everybody knew when to give up power and when to be at the bottom, who should be leading a utopian society next. All celebrated life and glorified the creation in the new paradise, maximizing the artistic and sports events every other weekend at the local council, district, state, and national level, extending paradise beyond physical boundaries for the transformation of the nation and the entire world, for celebrating life and exalting the creation glory.

# CHAPTER 69 ECHOES

"What is lacking in the world, and why are we struggling?" Echoes continued day in and out whenever I thought about why all cannot be celebrating life and why cannot we see everyone smiling. I guess that happens when you are in the zone of enlightenment. Once you have the light within you, it has to come out like a light tower lighting the darkness around it because light cannot be contained. Like we see the pathways when the light shines, I saw straightforward ways out of the darkness. If we choose to be in darkness, we wouldn't know the path out of the darkness. That is why the world is struggling because we have chosen darkness. We have decided to hold on to everything and get attached to everything, even though we are temporary. When we are in the darkness, there are no possible solutions to the acquired problems unless we choose to loosen whatever we have acquired and embrace the light again. We acquire problems simply by not knowing our purpose and mission and not connecting to our creator. Remember, nothing can exist in this world by itself; everything has a creator, and science tells us that without force or cause, there can be no presence of anything, not even the tiniest particle.

Everything not connected to the creator will not attain its full lifecycle and withers away after completely cutting itself off from the creator. Though the moment the creation connects with its creator, it returns to its life cycle, ultimately attaining some of its lost paths, there would be consequences for being in the darkness, like a significant cut in our hand leaving a scar for a long time even after getting healed. Sometimes the scar never fades away.

"Yet why do all those who walk in the light still suffer, face challenges, or lose the battles?" Again, an echo set the alarm in my mind. Immediately light shined upon me, "That is the process of building resilience, strength, character, and humility to go through a tougher terrain of life. Gold cannot shine unless it is put through the fire; an athlete has to work hard and perform to win medals. Therefore, the higher the purpose or the given mission, the more the struggles and defeats to win the ultimate crown of glory."

Nothing has been created without the infrastructure to perform and live its ultimate life. No cars were built before roads were available, airplanes were manufactured before airports were open, and mobile phones were created before mobile networks were available. Similarly, humans were created or existed only after everything was made available to live an ultimate life. And there is more than enough for every person to live in abundance.

All creations' life cycle depends on both nature and nurture. Nature provides for every life the inbuilt capacities, talent, and passion with mandatory processes, rules, and regulations. Then nurture promotes those capacities and skills to fulfill optimal life cycles based on environment, support, and adherence to the creator's processes, rules, and regulations. Like different cars have different capacities and inbuilt abilities, yet following the creator's methods of servicing them after running certain kilometers and driving them by following nurtured road safety ideals are essential to fulfill ultimate lifecycles.

Similarly, every human has unique inbuilt capacities, talents, and passions from nature. Nurture plays a vital role in developing those inbuilt talents, passion, and abilities by providing an ideal environment and opportunities throughout the different life stages by supporting the development of human virtues of kindness, honesty, generosity, compassion, justice, resilience, and self-control to live an ultimate lifecycle.

Every creator has warranties in place for every creation to fulfill its ultimate life cycle, and for those warranties to be applied, every product must go through the process defined by the creator. If any product is used beyond its stated capacities and purposes or misused by not handling as prescribed by the creator, it would lose its warranty and ultimately withers away without achieving its ultimate life cycle.

Similarly, humans have warranties and processes and protocols to maintain those warranties. The moment we do not follow those processes, obey the creator's rules and regulations or go beyond our capacities and purposes, we will lose our warranty and fail to live an ultimate life celebrating every moment.

Life is like driving a car on the road to reach our destination. If we follow all the ideal driving norms, obeying all road safety regulations like following the speed limit, safe distance, proper indications for turning and lane changing, stopping at the red light, and maintaining our car as per the manufacturer protocols, then we would safely reach our destination. Yet we wouldn't be traveling at the same speed from beginning to end as there could be road closures, accidents, traffic, rains, winds, humps, potholes, narrow roads, bridges, hills, and valleys, and sometimes we would take alternative routes to reach our destination. Similarly, ultimate life is all about following the ideal processes, though there would be hurdles, humps, delays, accidents, loss, and grief.

Every creation has a specific life span, and we, too, have a limited time for our life journey. Death can't be escaped, yet life lived with processes, rules, and regulations would provide content and a good end. A life lived with attachment, and accumulation would provide regrets and a sour end to life.

If we don't follow the traffic rules, there will be accidents that could be serious and injuring not only us but others as well. Similarly, if we don't mind life's rules of loving, kindness, humility, sharing, and caring, we will be in disorder, and the society around us will suffer. That is why there is so much hatred and violence today. It is time to wake up and follow life's simple rules.

# CHAPTER 70 WHO AM I?

I am an enigma. Unknown and yet known. I am myself, but I am you just as you are me. I am not my name. My identity moves beyond words, for I am the servant, the leader, and the motivator. I seek absolute truth to celebrate life in all circumstances and situations. I am the tree clinging to the edge of the exposed buffs, overlooking the wild tumultuous waves below, my roots exposed, still sprawling my limbs to the infinite sky. I care not for fame or even recognition. I choose to disconnect from the self to gain something much bigger than myself — everything. The whole. The source. The start. The end. The truth.

Who is Dave Sonsoil? You are, of course. You write this extraordinary novel; you have these ideas; you wrote these words. It is not a case of forgetting; it is a case of awakening. You are Dhaval Sonsoil. We are all Dhaval Sonsoil. Just as the universe can never belong to anyone, Earth, too, belongs only to itself. And as we are part of the Earth, and any perceived separation is just an illusion, we must remember that we are all one. We are the soil that our ancestors are buried in. We are the light that shines for others to walk out from the darkness. We are the salt that gives taste to the dishes. Distance is only an illusion and separation, a great trick we play upon ourselves for the sake of the experience of this great thing we call life.

But we are not separate. Even the sun, seemingly thousands of miles away, touches our skin through quantum tunneling. The sunlight does not start at the sun and ends at our faces. It is a constant that forms in rays, just as everything forms in rays and is infinite. We have to wake up to it. Again, to realize what we knew all along, everything is one.

And no creations are created for self; all products are designed for others' benefit and to serve others. The rivers don't drink their water, the trees don't eat their fruits, the cars don't travel empty for themselves, and the mobile phones don't connect with other phones for themselves. Any creation alone cannot fulfill its life cycle; all creations require communion with other creations to live their ultimate lives.

We all have our talents, just as every object, animal, and place has its essence and quality. We must stop comparing ourselves and things! We are all unique. In India, we have a word to honor the divine in oneself and another; Namaste! Imagine we all live like plants, sharing our fruitfulness, unique talent, outstanding creativity, and novel inventions! Then everyone in this world will have enough of what they want, to live in peace and prosperity!

Dhaval Sonsoil stands for worldwide peace, harmony, balance, justice, equality, and unity in diversity. The glory of nature is always waiting for us patiently to show its love and warmth, always expecting our return. It is time we woke up and realized that it is up to us to be this world's caregivers. We are all gifted, we are all talented, and we are all beautiful. The only thing we must do is wake up and see it. Like light shines for others, we can too shine the peace on others when we have peace within us through living a content and joyous life!

I believe in truth, honesty, in compassion. I believe in love. Eden on Earth is an idea, and it's a movement. We can all live on this planet peacefully, but we have to work towards that goal together. It is time we forge our traditions; we build a new world, a new system in which we can all be happy and live together not just now, not just for the next few generations, but forever. The world may be in chaos, but let's remember to support one another for everyone to live in peace and prosperity!

We can all make a positive change in the world. Every small action counts. We are all one. Let's work together to create a brighter future! I'm on a mission to rebuild the world, to restore peace and harmony with nature. The future is what we make it. We must believe in ourselves. We must continue to believe in a brighter future. We must continue believing in the power of the human spirit and connection. Every one of us has different instincts for different kinds of sports, art, craft, cinema, and other career fields! This is nature's creation glory for us; our uniqueness adds to the beautiful experience of living life on Earth!

It's time for a change! The world needs more people following their passions and making a difference. We all ought to have the freedom to find our talents. Together we can make it happen for all to have the freedom to find their passion and talent to live in peace and prosperity without bias for religion, caste, creed, and status! Remember, no one owns the Earth. The Earth holds us. It does not owe us anything, and all it asks in return for the gift of our existence is one thing only—gratitude. Wake up! Step outside and breathe the air deeply, listen to the rain, get lost watching the clouds, hug a tree, sing, laugh, meditate and rejoice! This world is to be experienced! This world is already our paradise for us to live in peace by sharing and caring!

Together, we can create great things. Together, we can change the world. Together we can celebrate life.

# CHAPTER 71 LOVE IS EVERYTHING

I woke up with a start. The window was slightly open, and the breeze blew through the gap, making the light white curtains dance like ghosts. I looked out the window and saw that everything was bathed in the pale light of dawn. It had rained overnight, so the landscape had a bluish tone; the trees and the fields were covered in a wet sheen. The pale river shimmered, and only a few birds gathered in the sky and dared to make a sound looking over the inundated paddy fields. The sun was low in the sky, casting a pearly white light upon the water and across the blue sky. There were no sounds of electric machines, no tractors, nothing but the gentle trickling of water. The air was soft and clean. As I saw it at that moment, the world was perfectly serene.

I gently got up from the bed by slowly removing the blanket over me and covering Asha with double folds for her to be warm. Her beautiful face shone like a mirror, and even in her sleep, her smiling face lighted my heart. Such mad was love that it had conquered everything, it had forgotten everything, it had healed everything, it had united everything, and it had provided everything.

After freshening up, I walked straight to the kitchen and washed all the vessels piled up in the sink. Then I started arranging the kitchen until I suddenly noticed the dosa (pancake) batter sneaking out from a bowl by lifting its lid. I panicked, yet I realized that batter would overflow if I didn't put it into a pan to make dosa. The kitchen became disarranged, trying to find the dosa pan, but I was determined that I shouldn't wake up Asha or wait for her. Until then, I wasn't required to do anything in the kitchen, and I had hardly any experience in the kitchen as I didn't like to be there. Though I had watched Asha making dosa, I didn't know the intricacies of cooking it. But today, everything changed without thinking, and my mind and hands moved all over the kitchen. I poured little oil on the pan and spread it with a cut onion, kept the pan on a stove, lit the burner, and poured the dosa batter. The first few dosas were a little burnt as I didn't know what intensity of flame it required to cook, but after a few more attempts, it looked like I had already mastered the art of dosa cooking in my first attempt at the kitchen. And I learned that love teaches everything, even though we had not tried it before.

I heard Asha's screech that something was on fire, and I realized that a burning smell had reached the bedroom. But that didn't put me off as I took a couple of dosa on a plate and tea straight to the bedroom. There were some loving murmurs from Asha, but her surprise that she, too, could have breakfast at the bedside overpowered everything else. "Hope you have not burnt the whole kitchen. Thank you, Dave. I didn't expect this; thank you for being my love," Asha's words inflated my swollen heart.

Such was the love; love doesn't wait for others to do something, it doesn't judge, it doesn't assign work to others, it inspires you to do everything even if you are tired, it allows you to hear even if you have done the correct thing, it doesn't ask "why should I do it?" or "what is there for me in it?" or "why can't you do it?".

Love is the foundation of the entire creation; therefore, love makes your content, shows your purpose, make us share and care, brings out passion and talent, discovers the unknown, and finds time to do things even if you feel you don't have time. Love doesn't argue, makes you hear everyone, makes you wish good and pray for enemies and ultimately love them; love makes you love everyone as they are, without judging them, instead showing the right path for their wrong actions.

"Wow, great dosa," said Asha, forgetting I had little role to play in the goodness of the dosa as she had made everything ready by mixing all the ingredients. Such is love; it forgets who has sowed the seed but celebrates the fruits, like a mother celebrating a child's birth ignoring the pain she has gone through.

Love made me and Asha do everything without assigning or rostering the work at home and in Paradise. True love rosters everything, the work we need to do, the words we need to speak, the actions we need to take, and the feelings we need to feel. If I got up early, I did all the work in the kitchen; if she came home early, she cooked that day. If I saw clothes piled up, I washed them, and if she noticed dust on the floor, she would sweep and vacuum. If she got angry and shouted, I kept quiet even if she was wrong. If I get mad and raise my voice, even if she is correct, she keeps quiet without any argument, and we tease each other about those angry episodes when we are in a good mood. True love made everything more peaceful and calm, making us go hand in hand wherever we go, meditate, pray, visit places of worship, connect to our creator and work together. Love developed respect for each other and gratitude for every moment to celebrate life joyfully.

Love is everything because nature's love provides us with everything. The air we breathe, the water we drink, the sun that gives us light, the rain that produces the yield, the plants, the trees, the fruits, the rivers, the seas, the animals, and so on. Nature does not judge anyone; it provides everything to everyone, whether worthy or unworthy because it loves everyone.

I, Asha, and Paradise experienced true love, a selfless love which reminded me of Saint Paul's first letter to Corinthians: "Love is patient; love is kind; love is not envious or boastful or arrogant or rude. It does not insist on its way; it is not irritable; it keeps no record of wrongs; it does not rejoice in wrongdoing but in truth. It bears all things, believes, hopes, endures all things, and love never ends."

Experiencing and living in love, a true love, selfless love, is truly and indeed enlightenment!

# CHAPTER 72 CELEBRATING LIFE IN EDEN

I had left Paradise searching for love and life and wandered everywhere to find it, but ultimately, I found love and life in Paradise itself. I realized wherever we may be, Eden exists then and there. We need not go searching for Eden. It is already here, all around us. It is here in the rivers, it's here in the trees, and it is here in the wind. It is here on Earth. And it has always been here. I didn't know what it was or how to experience it. All this time, we had convinced ourselves Eden was something distant, separate from us, when all we had to do was open our eyes and see and experience it by living in it. This is the glory of existence. Everything you see and hear and have the privilege of experiencing is Eden on Earth.

Eden on Earth at Paradise lives in complete balance with nature, never taking too much and never harming the environment. Eden on Earth is everywhere, and everyone and every society is part of it. It's all of us working together to create paradise on Earth. Everything and everyone at Paradise learned to embrace the unknown. We learned to enjoy having our beliefs challenged and broken and to rejoice in being lost. Only when we step into places we have never been before can we ever honestly hope to find anything. We reaped what we sowed. We sowed love, kindness, empathy, caring, and sharing and reaped peace, joy, togetherness, and prosperity for everyone to live in abundance!

Just as trees wear the snow, rain, and sun with the same dignity and produce fruits that provide nourishment and branches that give us shade when it is hot or wet, we at Paradise live our lives with dignity and bear the fruits of humility, generosity, and compassion in every situation. We were born to dance, sing and laugh and in doing so, we exercise gratitude for every moment we ever have and will ever indeed be given. Now we realize we didn't sing, dance, and laugh simultaneously. Indeed, it ought to be the accurate measure of happiness!

In Eden, calmness, harmony, and balance are not lofty, unreachable ideals but a normal part of everyday existence. This is how we brought the world back to balance. We celebrate life daily by connecting to our creator, which is what life is supposed to be. A grand occasion, an excellent reason for meaning and happiness in and of itself.

The value of a tree is measured by its usefulness or fruits, not by its height and spread. Similarly, our value is measured by our usefulness and fruitfulness for society and the world, not by our wealth and status! If all eight billion people play their specific roles and purposes, the world will be victorious and live in peace and prosperity! Remember, we are all on this Earth to live happily in all circumstances and to celebrate as one big, winning team!

There is much chaos in the world now but remember, just before sunrise, there is a night. Positive change will happen! We must keep positive and walk in the light filling our minds with hope and inspiration! We are mindful at Paradise by listening to the rustling of the leaves in the trees and birds singing in their nests to experience life. We turned back from the path of pollution and returned to nature. We got all the necessary answers and will find everything in nature through our hearts! For we, too, are not separate from this planet. We don't just live in Eden. We are the Eden.

At Paradise, the transformation doesn't just happen from the outside. Just as we get dressed every day before leaving the house, we wrap our hearts and minds with new thoughts, love, and peace. Just as every butterfly must leave its cocoon and every bird must leave its nest, we at Paradise left our old ways behind and chose to fly in freedom.

At Paradise, the peace lovers are well-organized, as Martin Luther King proclaimed, just as those who love violence. We made a difference and became the change we wanted to see in Paradise. We built a new paradise, a new society, a new world, and a new age. We defined our destiny and decided what to make of this Earth. This is the power of human beings. This is the power of consciousness that we can think, imagine, and act; we will never forget this!

At Paradise, we experience life in all its wonder. We live as if life itself is a dance. Every day we wake up, breathe life, and experience the joy of being. We wake up and see the world's beauty before it's too late. We share our specialty in our way and know that there is only one "ME." We changed Paradise by controlling our minds, and now we live without fear, selfishness, and greed.

Paradise is in complete harmony. We achieved our dream, and now we know what it takes to achieve it. If all the world's people work together, we can achieve great things. The future is not set in stone. We make our future, and we believe in a bright future. We asked ourselves what we wanted our future to look like. We understood ourselves first, our role in our family, neighborhood, and society, the words we speak, and the path we walk. We looked not outward but inward. In Paradise, we live with joy in our hearts, compassion in all our dealings with others, kindness in our thoughts, and gentleness in our actions to celebrate life at all times. We became selfless, humble, and simple with loving and caring, and change embraced Paradise for everyone to live in peace and prosperity.

A flicker of static, and I felt as if I had awoken yet again, woken from wakefulness, to see the past and future played before me like an analog movie. Sometimes in my life, I collapsed. Sometimes in my life, I shone. But regardless, I lived. I connected. I experienced love, true love. I experienced and celebrated life. I am that fallen bird with the broken wing, now flying. I saw my daughter tie a blue ribbon around the love-heart tree along with Asha. I saw petals blowing gently in the breeze. Dandelion seeds floated in the wind, dancing electrically as they flittered through the air, as I felt my eyes closing. I let go of everything. And I knew. And I knew. That I had reached the pinnacle of pinnacles. I had given up everything because I didn't need everything.

[illegible] our family, neighbourhood, and [illegible] the words we spoke and the path we walk. We looked out toward [illegible] inward. In Paradise [illegible] live with [illegible] our hearts' compassion [illegible] all our decisions, with [illegible] kindness in our thoughts, and gentleness in our actions, to celebrate [illegible] at all times. We become selfless, humble and simple with loving and caring, and change [illegible] Paradise [illegible] everyone to live in peace and [illegible]

[illegible] of sadness [illegible] but [illegible] past and future prayers [illegible] Sometimes [illegible] my life I collapsed sometimes [illegible] regardless, I lived. [illegible] I experienced a [illegible] celebrated life. I am that [illegible] with the broken [illegible] I saw my daughter [illegible] around [illegible] along with [illegible] blowing gently in the breeze. Dandelion seeds [illegible] in the wind, dancing delicately as they [illegible] through the [illegible] I let go of everything. And I knew. And I knew that I had reached the pinnacle of [illegible] I had given [illegible] because I didn't [illegible] everything.

# About Eden on Earth

Eden on Earth is an epic romance and magical realist adventure set in India. In the quest to find 'life' after a series of setbacks and tragedies, Dhaval Sonsoil embarks upon something much more than a 'living life' with coming of age philosophy, finally unearthing a 'celebrating life' to reunite with his soul mate Asha after many years.

The novel has an overarching sense of beauty (especially concerning the natural world) and a human tragedy. Spiritual enlightenment is the main theme but nothing religious. The story is eclectic and includes many different cultural vibes and spiritual and philosophical ideas.